How to
Haunt a House

Published in the United States by Random House, Inc., New York,
and simultaneously in Canada by Random House of Canada Limited, Toronto.

Library of Congress Catalog Card Number: 94-67184

ISBN: 0-679-86742-2

Manufactured in the United States of America 1 2 3 4 5 6 7 8 9 0

BOOks! is an imprint of Random House, Inc./MagicCom, Inc.

HOW TO
HAUNT A HOUSE

By Dan Witkowski

Illustrations by Jack Lindstrom

Cover illustration by Jim Rownd

With special material by Philip Morris, Dennis Phillips, John Shepard, and Bev Bergeron

Special thanks to the Morris Costume Company, Charlotte, North Carolina

Random House 🏠 New York

To mischief-makers and trick-or-treaters everywhere

CONTENTS

MASTER OF THE HOUSE OF TERROR

Are there nasty noises in your basement? Screeching bats in the belfry? Did the lights suddenly go out...and isn't that the sound of heavy footsteps climbing the creaking stairs?

No problem. Your wide-eyed friends are starting to panic, but everything's working out just the way you planned...because you're the Count of the Castle, Master of this House of Terror!

Maybe you're in the market for some fun pranks to spring on your big sister or little brother. Perhaps you're looking for ideas to pull off a major freak show for your school, club, or for Halloween. Or how about a full-scale ghostly gathering to celebrate your birthday? Whether your plans are ghoulishly grand or sinister but simple, in the pages of this book you'll find exactly what you need to know.

From the simplest recipes for morbid morsels to the most fantastic illusions, *How to Haunt a House* is a Pandora's box of ghoulish delights. Follow the book's step-by-step instructions and you'll quickly become a master illusionist who can:

■ **Execute chilling illusions and tricks**

■ **Create frightful costumes and makeup**

■ **Produce dazzling special lighting effects**

■ **Develop a recorded library of spooky sound effects**

■ **Mastermind an evening's worth of haunting entertainment**

■ **Transform your lawn into a boneyard and your house into a monster mausoleum**

Most of the effects and stunts described in these pages can be done with items found around the house, though a few will require a trip to the store. But the most important ingredient for having fun with these projects is your imagination. Using the ideas from *How to Haunt a House* as a guide, you'll be able to create your own one-of-a-kind effects and tricks and set the perfect mood for creating an absolutely unforgettable house of horrors.

HAUNTED HOUSE DO'S AND DON'TS

Any spook will tell you there's a right way and a wrong way to run a house of horrors. Vampires are so freaked out by mirrors, for example, that if you leave one hanging around they'll lock themselves away in the nearest empty coffin.

You want your haunted house to be frightful yet fun; a little sickening, perhaps, but not too gross, and definitely safe. As you hatch your plans, put yourself in your guests' shoes. (Who knows, the next person to get spooked might very well be you!) Nearly everyone likes a good scare every now and then, but nobody likes getting slimed with mystery muck, being completely grossed out, or getting truly terrified. And you must operate your haunted house and plan your pranks so there's no chance anyone will get hurt.

Here are some guidelines that you should follow to make sure everyone has a ghoulish good time:

■ **Get a parent to be your partner in crime.** Ask a parent or a responsible adult to help you with your plans. You'll need a little assistance from a grown-up to pull off some of the projects in this book. For sure, any plans that involve houseguests (including your friends) or projects that change the appearance of your house or yard will need an okay... your parents do, after all, pay the rent. Also, have an adult check out your exhibits before your guests arrive to be extra sure they're safe. This is a must!

■ **Beware of fire.** Even Frankenstein's monster was deathly afraid of fire, and with good reason. Fire is truly frightening...and deadly...stuff. Follow the directions in this book and learn to use flashlights and special light bulbs for making eerie effects. Never use matches, candles, cigarette lighters, gasoline, gas burners, open flames of any kind, or materials that easily burn in your haunted house. Use fire retardant materials or make materials fireproof (see page 12 for details). Tell adults or anyone else who smokes that you'll cast a spell on them if they don't put out their cigarettes before entering. Keep a fire extinguisher and first aid kit handy.

■ **Don't get zapped.** Make sure all electrical cords are safely out of the way so no one will trip over them. Keep all electrical appliances far away from water.

■ **Cutting up without getting cut.** Never use real glass, glass mirrors, knives, axes, razors, other sharp objects, or weapons of any kind. It is too easy for accidents to happen, especially in the dark.

■ **Keeping 'em in the (almost) dark.** Dimming the lights and using flashlights can be great fun. Plunging people into complete darkness, however, is dangerous and can be terrifying. Remember, you know what lurks in the shadows (at least you may think you know), but your friends will have no idea what to expect. Make sure there's enough light so everyone can see where they're going at all times and be certain that the way out of every room is marked or clearly visible. Glow-in-the-dark tape works well for this (see page 61). Mark all exits clearly with EXIT signs.

■ **Obstacles and hazards.** Make sure that there are no objects on the floor people could fall over and that your guests can't go near windows, stairways, open doors, or other hazards. Keep the walking paths clear.

■ **Treat little kids kindly.** It's easy to forget how scary things can be for young children, so be sure to have them walk with an adult if they explore your haunted house, and don't do anything to frighten them.

■ **Rules for ghouls.** Set up and enforce basic safety rules for your haunted house, including: no running, hitting, pushing, or grabbing anyone else.

■ **Permits and insurance.** If you are operating a haunted house that is open to the public in order to raise money for an organization, or if you charge admission, you will need insurance and you may need a permit. Talk to an adult about this. He or she will need to get city officials, the police, and the fire department involved from the start.

9

NOOKS AND CRANNIES FOR CRABBY SPOOKS

Dracula had his castle in Transylvania. The Mummy had his tomb. And your first job as spook-house master is to find the right house to haunt. There's probably a perfect nook or cranny right under your nose...the trick is to use your impish imagination. You also should get an okay from a parent or responsible adult before you deck the halls with fearsome hangings.

PROPS AND PREPARATION

Places to look for building the spook house of your dreams:

■ *GARAGES* provide great open space for elaborate scenes and for hanging horrible objects from the ceiling or walls.

■ *BASEMENTS,* especially unfinished ones, are naturally spooky and can work well for grand spook-house plans.

■ *ATTICS* filled with old trunks and forgotten objects are as wonderfully scary as basements.

■ *YOUR BEDROOM*—if your parents agree—may suit your sinister schemes, too.

■ With permission, *FAMILY ROOMS* or *PLAYROOMS* may be a perfect places for horrible haunts.

■ *A LARGE TENT* erected in your backyard can provide a spooky setting for a seánce, especially at night.

■ *A PARTY ROOM* in your apartment building might work well for a haunted happening.

■ *MEETING ROOMS* or *LUNCH-ROOMS* at schools, churches, or neighborhood recreation centers are perfect for ghoulish group events.

COMING SOON
HAUNTED HOUSE

PETRIFED PARTIES, HAUNTED HAPPENINGS

Maybe your birthday is approaching. Or a chill in the air signals that Halloween is on its way. Or maybe it's just time for an outrageous party that you and your friends will never forget. Whatever the occasion, when the spirit moves you to put together a haunted happening, here are the main ingredients for creating a spectacularly spooky event.

PROPS AND PREPARATION

■ *INSIDIOUS INVITATIONS.* When Dracula pops out of an envelope made to look like a coffin, your friends will know that something sinister is afoot. Or you may consider cutting out a paper-doll mummy and printing the date, time, and place of the event. Your friends will have to unwrap the mummy from the paper strips in which you've entwined him in order to learn his curse!

■ *FRIGHTENING FOOD.* Serve food fit for ghouls at your party so your friends will freak even before things get really scary. Refer to the Frightful Feast section (page 94) for instructions on how to produce such demented (if not delicious) delights as Tarantula Tacos and Eyeballs and Entrails.

■ *GHOST STORIES.* A visit to the deep, dank recesses of your neighborhood or school library may produce some ghastly literature for you to share with your friends. "Did ya hear the one about the vanishing hitchhiker...?"

■ *GHOULISH GAMES.* Besides telling stories about themselves, what do you suppose zombies and werewolves do on nights when the weather is too foul to prowl? Pin the Spider in Its Web is a favorite time-killer played much the same way that normal folks play Pin the Tail on the Donkey.

Mad Hypnotist is another great ghastly game: pick one playing card as the "Hypnotist card." Have everyone select and look at a card, then turn it face down on the pile. The person who draws the "Hypnotist card" goes on a silent rampage by winking at his or her victims. The victims count to ten and then fall into everlasting sleep.

The winner of each round is either the Mad Hypnotist (who must do in the entire group without being detected) or the detective (a potential victim who catches the Mad Hypnotist in action and accuses him or her

of the crimes). Inaccurate accusers are gone from the game.

■ *DASTARDLY DECORATIONS.* To help your guests get into the proper frame of mindlessness, dim the lights and play a little spooky background music (see page 57). Then add a liberal dose of cobwebs (page 42) and a colony or two of hanging bats (page 13) or scampering rats (page 16).

You may even want to include some special lighting effects (pages 58–71), a little fog floating about the floor (page 31), or even a grand illusion or two.

■ *GHOULISH GIFTS.* Think of creepy-crawly presents to give your guests as party favors. Shrunken heads are always popular at these gatherings (make one out of painted, sculpted plastic foam with fake hair attached). Leftover party decorations make good parting gifts, too.

These are just a few tips to get you started thinking about a party that everyone will be talking about. Just remember, don't go overboard trying to gross people out. After all, they are your guests.

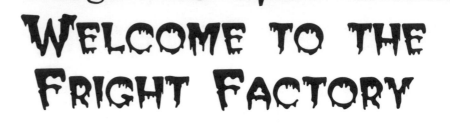

WELCOME TO THE FRIGHT FACTORY

PROPS AND PREPARATION

To avoid an industrial disaster in the Fright Factory, follow these guidelines:

■ Most of the materials you'll need can be found around the house. A few will require a trip to a hardware store, craft store, grocery store, fabric store, or theatrical supply store.

■ Make sure you ask an adult to help you when construction calls for the use of tools such as a glue gun, paint, or a hammer.

■ Use fire retardant materials whenever possible (an adult can help you find these). When you must use cloth, wood, or other burnable substances, have an adult help you apply a fire retardant spray on the finished product.

Chemical fire retardant compounds can be purchased at most theatrical supply stores. Follow the directions on the package for mixing and application.

Note: Have a parent or other adult help you prepare and apply fire retardant mixtures to fabric. Properly dispose of any unused mixture. Proper safety precautions should be used at all times.

Okay, Igor, it's time to roll up your tattered sleeves and start manufacturing mayhem. The Fright Factory is where it all happens. And this chapter provides you with the step-by-step instructions you'll need to crank out the kind of creepy creations that will make your haunted happenings a hit.

All the bone-chilling objects and creatures you will learn to make can be used by themselves or assembled into horrific combinations. (Check out the Scenes of Terror chapter that starts on page 90 to see how you can bring everything together for frightful fun.)

FEARSOME, FLAPPING BATS

Half bird and half rat, dark as the night and ugly as sin, what a wonderful creature is the bat! There are even several kinds that suck the blood of other animals for their dinner. They're called...you guessed it...vampire bats. You'll want to have a colony or two of these twitching creatures dangling from the rafters of your house of horrors.

PROPS AND PREPARATION

YOU WILL NEED...

- *The bat design on this page*
- *Tracing paper*
- *Stiff cardboard*
- *Scissors*
- *Black paint or marking pen*
- *Fake dark brown fur (from a fabric store)*
- *Household glue*

HOW TO DO IT...

Trace the bat design on this page and use it as an outline for making the body and wings. Cut your paper along the tracing lines, then use your tracing-paper bat to mark lines on stiff cardboard, which you can cut out. Paint the cardboard wings black and attach the fake fur to the body with glue for a life-like feel.

Your bat colony can be hung from exposed rafters, in the basement or garage, or against some other dark background. Use "invisible" black thread or, better yet, thin strands of black elastic material that will let the bats jiggle and twitch when they're touched.

You can make your bat fly by tying it with black thread to a long stick (also painted black) that is dangled in midair by a well-hidden assistant.

13

Giant Spiders & Terrifying Tarantulas

Did you know that most of the 30,000 carnivorous spider species on earth have poisonous bites? Some, like the Black Widow, are so nasty they kill their own mates. Certainly, you'll want plenty of these charming creatures skittering about the walls of your haunted house and clinging to webs in every corner.

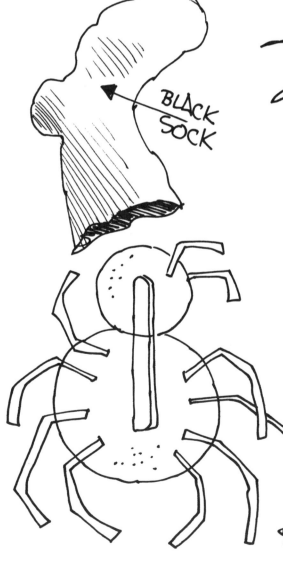

BLACK SOCK

PROPS AND PREPARATION

FOR EACH SPIDER YOU WILL NEED...

- *2 plastic foam balls, 1 baseball-sized and 1 grapefruit-sized (sold in craft stores)*
- *2 black nylon stockings or 2 black socks*
- *Scissors*
- *An ice cream bar stick (eat the ice cream first!)*
- *A package of long black pipe cleaners (or white ones that can be painted black)*
- *Household glue*
- *Black thread*

GLUE

HOW TO DO IT...

Cover both plastic foam balls with the socks. Push the ball all the way to the toe of the sock. Tie a knot in the sock and cut away the excess.

Use the stick to attach the small ball to the large ball by poking the stick halfway through both balls.

Insert eight pipe cleaners into the big plastic foam ball and bend them to look like legs.

Cut two pieces of pipe cleaner about two inches long, and attach them with glue to the small ball (the spider's head) to form curved spider "whiskers."

Spiders and tarantulas can be suspended from the ceiling, placed in webs, or dangled in front of unsuspecting visitors by using black thread and attaching it to the spider's body.

Make up several spiders and scatter them among the bats and rats in your chamber of horrors.

SPINNING SPIDER WEBS

Since your haunted house is more heavily occupied by the creatures of the night than those that live by the light of day, cobwebs should be found in every corner and suspended from each door frame. Luckily for you, since you'd have trouble spinning them on your own, you can easily make weblike material or buy fake cobwebs for a few dollars at a theatrical supply store.

PROPS AND PREPARATION

YOU WILL NEED...

- *Cheesecloth (from a fabric or grocery store)*
- *Black or gray dye, or red, blue, and green food coloring mixed together so they become almost black*
- *Tape*

HOW TO DO IT...

Using all eight of your arms, remove some of the threadlike strands of the cheesecloth until it appears fragile and weblike.

With an adult's help, soak the cheesecloth in black or gray dye, or the red, blue, and green mixture of food coloring, then hang it outside to dry so that it does not drip on the floor (it will stain).

Attach the completed webs to the walls, doors, or room corners with tape.

Rats, Rats, and More Rats

Rats, lovely rats. These teeming little creatures were responsible for spreading the Black Death...a plague that killed off a quarter of the European population in the 1300s. With this history, surely rodents should be well represented in your house of horrors. An occasional rat racing across the floor or sharing a meal with some friends in the corner will do wonders for setting the mood.

PROPS AND PREPARATION

YOU WILL NEED...

- *Several old, long black socks*
- *Stuffing (more socks, cotton, or other light fabrics)*
- *Black thread*
- *Black wire or cable*
- *Black pipe cleaners for legs (or white ones painted black)*
- *Remnants of black felt for ears*
- *Buttons for eyes*
- *Needle and thread*

HOW TO DO IT...

Start by stuffing the socks. You can give the bodies a realistic shape by stuffing more material in the bottom half than near the head. You can also tie black thread or twist wire around the thinner parts of the body to help get and maintain the proper shape.

Once the body has been formed, cut the sock off at the base of the tail and tie the opening closed so the cable tail sticks out. Fold the pipe cleaners several times so that they resemble legs and insert them in the proper places.

Cut out the black felt for the ears and attach with pipe cleaners poked through the top of the head. Last, sew the buttons on for eyes.

I've Been Slimed!

PROPS AND PREPARATION

YOU WILL NEED...

- Lime-flavored gelatin
  (available at grocery stores)

OR

- 2 cups of cornstarch
- 1 cup of water
- A few drops of green food coloring
- Large bowl

HOW TO DO IT...

Green gelatin has the advantage of being edible, in case you want to demonstrate your fearlessness in the face of hostile spirits. Make according to the instructions on the box, and leave piles of it in scooped-out clumps in appropriate places around the house (that is, places that your parents say are okay).

The cornstarch, water, and green food coloring mixture actually has a wonderful slimy texture that's more like real ectoplasm. But you won't want to snarf it down in a show of reckless courage. It also can stain fabrics, so be careful to leave it only on plastic or protected surfaces (check with an adult).

As your friends walk through your haunted house, invite them to touch the ectoplasm you have in a bowl. As they squeeze the gooey mess, it will change from liquid to solid, and to then liquid again. It's really gross!

Always provide a slime towel for them to wipe excess ectoplasm from their hands.

Your friends will be itching to call the ghost patrol after they discover a few well-placed deposits of gooey, dripping, glowing, lime-green ectoplasm. Pointing out these disgusting ghost droppings is a great way to introduce the idea that your house is inhabited by some less-than-tidy creatures with one foot in this world and one in the next. One thing to keep in mind, however, is that you'll need to find places to put the stuff that won't make your parents keel over and croak.

RATTLESNAKE EGGS

As guests pass through your haunted house, offer to show them one of the most unusual things in your creepy collection... some genuine, tiny rattlesnake eggs. When they open the envelope containing the eggs, a loud buzzing reverberates throughout the room. This one is sure to send them through the roof!

PROPS AND PREPARATION

YOU WILL NEED...

- *Business-size envelope (9 1/2" x 4 3/8")*
- *Sheet of stiff paper (8 1/2" x 11")*
- *2 medium-weight rubber bands*
- *Metal washer about the size of a quarter*
- *Stapler*
- *Black marking pen*

HOW TO DO IT...

Use the black marking pen to write on the outside of the envelope such things as... "Caution," "Danger," "Do Not Touch," "Rattlesnake Eggs Inside."

Attach the washer to the rubber bands, then staple the two rubber bands to the middle of the paper (as shown). Carefully wind up the washer about twenty times, until the rubber bands are completely twisted.

Fold up the paper into thirds and carefully place it inside the envelope, making sure you do not let up on the tension of the rubber bands.

When your victim opens the envelope to remove the folded paper, the rubber bands quickly unwind, causing the washer to spin and vibrate against the paper, producing a rattling sound.

It is worth the trouble to make several envelopes so you won't have to constantly rewind the rubber bands.

SKULL AND BONES

Any bonehead knows that a haunted house is incomplete without at least a few skeleton parts lying about. A skull grinning down from the mantel, a collar bone lying in the corner being chewed on by rats. It's those little touches that make all the difference in helping a ghoul feel right at home.

PROPS AND PREPARATION

YOU WILL NEED...

- *White sculpting clay (from a craft supply store)*
- *Bones (from a grocery store or butcher shop)*

HOW TO DO IT...

Use your head, (but not as a mold) and apply a little creativity with your fingertips, and your skull will take shape nicely. The illustration on this page can serve as a model for your sculpture.

Also, the butcher at your neighborhood grocery store is likely to have some splendid bones for you to pick from. Large beef bones are likely to be your best bet.

If the bones are fresh, you may want to ask an adult to help you remove any meat and then bake them long enough to achieve that dried-out, well-aged look.

19

You will need an adult's help for this project.

YOU WILL ALSO NEED...

- *3 cardboard file boxes with removable or hinged lids*
- *Masking tape*
- *Large corrugated cardboard box or sheet*
- *Scissors*
- *Black or brown poster paint, or 3 yards of black felt or velour fabric (from a fabric store)*
- *Paintbrushes*
- *Thin foam-rubber padding (from a fabric store)*
- *White taffeta fabric (from a fabric store)*
- *Old pillow*
- *Hot glue gun*
- *Aluminum foil*

HOW TO DO IT...

Set the three file boxes end-to-end so they form a longer coffin shape. Cut off the ends that are touching each other to make one long box.

Connect the open (cut-off) ends and tape the insides to hold the boxes together where they join. (Follow the illustration on this page).

If the boxes have hinged lids, make sure you tape the boxes together so their lids open from the same side. If you need to make a lid for your coffin, have an adult use the scissors to cut the large cardboard box or sheet into a lid. Tape the lid to the top edge of one long side of the coffin.

Paint the coffin black or ask an adult to help you use the hot glue gun to attach black material to the coffin's sides and lid. With the help of an adult, cut the foam rubber to line the inside of the coffin, then cover the rubber with taffeta.

With an adult's help, use the hot glue gun to attach the taffeta to the top of the coffin. Wrap the pillow in taffeta and tape the material together on the back side.

Finally, form fake handles out of aluminum foil and use the glue gun to attach them to the sides of the coffin (don't try to lift the coffin with the handles).

COFFINS

You'd be amazed how handy it can be to have a few well-made coffins lying around your house of horrors. They're wonderful for storing excess rats and spiders. They make great hiding places when you simply must have a few moments to yourself. And they're essential for creating the marvelous kind of dreary, dismal mood called for in your graveyard (see pages 51 to 53), funeral parlor (page 90), or haunted attic (page 93).

REST IN PIECES

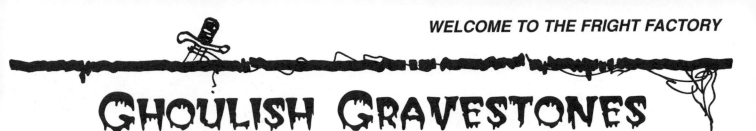

GHOULISH GRAVESTONES

Gravestones, cracked and faded in the pale moonlight, sticking out of the ground at odd angles as if they were rooted in some dark underworld.... It's enough to give you the shivers. Not only do they create a terrifically spooky effect, gravestones are also great ghoulish fun because you get to write whatever you want on them. Create sidesplitting epitaphs for your friends and family. Who knows, you may even get a chuckle out of the Grim Reaper himself, if he happens by.

PROPS AND PREPARATION

YOU WILL NEED...

- *Heavy-duty cardboard*
- *Scissors*
- *Paints or marking pens*
- *Old faded boards*
- *Plywood sheets, 1/4" or 1/2" thick, each 3' x 2'*
- *A jigsaw
  (Note: Operating a jigsaw is not kid's stuff. Have an adult do your cutting.)*
- *Granite fleckstone spray finish (from a hardware or paint store)*
- *Shovel*

HOW TO DO IT...

Quick and easy gravestones can be made of cardboard decorated with paint or marking pens.

If you want the gravestones to last several years, use weathered old planks nailed in the shape of a cross, or plywood cut into different interesting shapes (see illustrations) on a jigsaw. Ask a grown-up to operate the saw, though, or things may get really ugly!

Make your gravestones longer than needed so you can bury them in the ground. The granite fleckstone spray finish will give them a realistic stone-like look.

When you place the stones in the ground, have a few leaning at odd angles to give the boneyard that all-important rundown look.

If your parents don't object, place dead, dry leaves in front of some of the markers to look like freshly filled graves! Place a shovel next to one of the graves to complete the effect.

WELCOME TO THE FRIGHT FACTORY

DEAD DUMMIES

At first it may be a little hard to imagine how a stiff could be the life of the party, but think about it: Say what you like to this guy and he won't talk back. He doesn't pig out on the snacks. And, most important, if left lying in an unexpected place, he's bound to generate more than his share of excitement.

PROPS AND PREPARATION

YOU WILL NEED...

- An old shirt, a pair of pants, boots, and rubber gloves (flesh-colored gloves are best)
- Safety pins (12)
- Old flesh-colored nylon stocking or pair of pantyhose
- Paper towels, cloth towels, and rags for stuffing
- Paint or marking pens
- A hat or wig

HOW TO DO IT...

Stuff the shirt and pants with old rags or towels and tuck the shirt into the pants, securing it with safety pins. Stuff the gloves and attach them to the shirt sleeves with safety pins. Stuff the boots and jam the pant legs into them.

Stuff the nylon stocking with paper towels and mold it with your hands into a head shape. Paint a face on the stocking...as ghastly as you like...and add glasses or a mustache.

Top things off with a wig or a hat or both. If you like, you can even add a fright mask for the face.

Here's a fun dead dummy trick. To get the most mileage from it, have one stuffed dummy lying around that your guests can discover first. Then have a second—live—person, dressed up as a dummy, hidden in a more out-of-the-way place. Have him appear as lifeless as his rag-stuffed cousin—until, that is, everyone is gathered in close. Then have him suddenly come roaring to life.

PROPS AND PREPARATION

YOU WILL NEED...

- Large sheet of corrugated cardboard (about 2' x 4'), like the kind cut from boxes for large appliances, or a sheet of light foam core board (available from art stores)

- Black or brown poster paint and a brush

- Aluminum foil

- About 3 dozen (36) pointed sugar ice cream cones (it's best if they each have paper wrapped around them)

- Pencil

- Ruler

- Hot glue gun

> Note: Have an adult assist you with the glue gun so you don't get burned or permanently glued to your bed of spikes!

HOW TO DO IT...

Paint the cardboard or foam core board with poster paint. With the ruler and pencil, mark the places for the "spikes"—four rows of nine spikes running the length of the board works well. Tear off pieces of aluminum foil about eight inches long and wrap them around the cones.

Smooth out wrinkles so the cones look like metal and tuck extra foil inside the cone so it sits flat when placed on the open end. Use the glue gun to attach the cones to the board.

You can't have anyone actually lie on the bed of spikes, because the cones would be crushed into crumbs, but you can stand it against the wall or have an adult help you hang it from the ceiling—it will do wonders to create a perfectly sinister sleep-inducing mood.

BED OF SPIKES

On those rare occasions when you catch sight of a spook in the early morning, ask him how he slept. If he had a good night's rest, chances are he'll say that he nestled down for the night on a bed of gleaming metal spikes. As any ghoul knows, it's a dreamy way to sleep. Follow these instructions to make your own coffin-cozy bed of spikes.

HAUNTED HANDS

You'll probably need a few extra hands to put your haunted house together. When the work is done, it's not a bad idea to leave them lying around...they do wonders for the atmosphere.

PROPS AND PREPARATION

YOU WILL NEED...

- **Rubber gloves shaped like real hands (such as those sold for washing dishes)**
- **Plaster of Paris**
- **Flesh-colored paint**
- **Scissors**
- **Fake fur**
- **Household glue**

HOW TO DO IT...

Fill the rubber gloves with plaster of Paris, tie off the open ends, and suspend them from the ceiling of your garage to dry.

When the plaster is hard, paint each glove with flesh-colored paint and glue on fake fur to make the arms look hairy.

SPIRIT BANNERS

PROPS AND PREPARATION

YOU WILL NEED...

- ■ *2 yards of black felt or velour (from a fabric store)*
- ■ *Luminescent (glow-in-the-dark) paint (from a theatrical supply store)*
- ■ *2 wooden slats (one 5' long and one 3' long) nailed together to form a T*
- ■ *A few small nails*
- ■ *Hammer*
- ■ *Stapler*
- ■ *Fan*

HOW TO DO IT...

Black felt or velour makes a great "invisible" backdrop on which you can create ghosts of any size or shape using luminescent paint. Create a simple wooden T-shaped frame to support your shimmering, rippling ghost.

Expose the painted ghost to light for at least ten minutes so the ghost will light up in the dark. You can use the banner inside or out (if it's dark enough). With the right touch, you can cause it to ripple and sway...and the ghost will appear to fly. The trick to bringing the ghost to life is to move the wooden supporting frame by hand, position a fan out of sight so it blows against the cloth, or expose the banner to naturally haunting breezes.

Your haunted house will be deliciously dismal with a handful of lost and lonely spirits floating about. Create the proper mood by telling your friends a story about who the ghosts are and how they've come to haunt the place. Then activate a spirit banner...a glow-in-the-dark spook painted on "invisible" black felt...hiding in a dark corner or a dimly lit closet. When these dead start to walk, the living will surely balk!

STIFF STIFFS

Close cousins to the spirit banners, stiff stiffs are free to roam wherever they please, glowing as brightly as the moon and making the hair of every person they meet stand on end. Though they're made of cheesecloth, there ain't nothin' cheesy about these critters.

PROPS AND PREPARATION

YOU WILL NEED...

- ■ *2 pieces of cheesecloth, each measuring about 72" x 36" (from a fabric or grocery store)*
- ■ *Water and small bottle of household glue*
- ■ *2 balloons with strings*
- ■ *Newspapers*
- ■ *Luminescent (glow-in-the-dark) paint (from a theatrical supply store)*
- ■ *Black marking pen*
- ■ *Fishing line or black thread*
- ■ *2 large buttons*

HOW TO DO IT...

Cut the cheesecloth into two pieces, each measuring about two yards long by one yard wide. Then dip each piece in a mixture of one part household glue to one part warm water. Crisscross and drape each piece over an inflated balloon tied to a piece of string and attached to the ceiling. Mold the cheesecloth around the balloon to make a nice round shape, but let the bottom end dry in a ragged formation. Make sure to place newspapers underneath the balloon to catch any dripping glue. When the material dries, paint the stiff creatures with luminescent (glow-in-the-dark) paint. Use a black marking pen to add eyes and a mouth.

After the paint has dried, pop the balloon. Attach the black thread or fishing line to the ghosts by making a hole in the top of the head, threading the line through the hole, and tying it to a button inside the head. Now all you have to do is dangle your ghosts from the rafters after the luminescent paint has been exposed to light (for at least 10 minutes), so it will glow.

Cheesecloth ghosts suspended on practically invisible black thread are light and airy—perfect for drifting through dimly lit rooms. Try floating one toward an unsuspecting friend as he or she first walks in the door. Or how about an entire ghost family floating down a flight of stairs?

BOBBING BOOS

These unearthly spirits drift with the air currents and float up the stairs. Give them a chance and they'll slip up the chimney and be gone into the night, where they really belong.

PROPS AND PREPARATION

YOU WILL NEED...

- *Cheesecloth, measuring about 72" x 36" (from a fabric or grocery store)*
- *Helium-filled balloons (white is best) on strings*
- *Fan (optional)*
- *White thread*
- *Black marking pen*

HOW TO DO IT...

Bobbing Boos are so simple, they're a hoot to make. Just drape a layer of cheesecloth (about two yards long and one yard wide for each ghost) over a helium-filled balloon.

Gather the cheesecloth at the bottom of the balloon where the string is attached and tie it with the white thread. Then draw a gruesome face on the cloth with your black marking pen. Presto! You're in the spook business.

These bobbing beauties can be hidden, jack-in-the-box style, inside a chest or box to surprise whoever opens the lid. Or tie a row of them together and let the breeze from an open window or a hidden fan send them bobbing.

You may even want to have them bobbing up from behind furniture to keep your guests guessing which spook will pop up at them.

27

THE GRUMPY GREMLIN

Gremlins are short, green, and generally unpleasant creatures that seem always to have fallen out of bed on the wrong side after having slept not a wink. In other words, a gremlin would be perfect company for the other nasty spooks in your haunted house.

PROPS AND PREPARATION

YOU WILL NEED...

- *Sheet of plywood or fiber board about 2' x 4' x 1/8" thick*
- *Jigsaw (Note: Have an adult operate this)*
- *2 yards of black felt or velour fabric (available from a fabric store)*
- *Household glue*
- *Sawhorse*
- *Old children's clothing and shoes (clothes for a 1- to 3-year-old work well; a solid-color (green) kid's sweat suit is ideal)*
- *Rags or paper towels for stuffing the clothes*
- *Staple gun (Note: Have an adult help you)*
- *A grumpy, but willing, assistant*
- *Green theatrical makeup (from a theatrical supply store)*

HOW TO DO IT...

Have an adult cut out sections in the plywood for a head and two hands (see illustration) with a jigsaw. Cover the board with black felt and glue the felt to the board. Cut slits in the felt for the head and hand holes. Prop the board against the sawhorse so it is standing upright.

Stuff the clothes (a shirt and pants) with rags or paper towels. Have an adult attach the stuffed shirt and pants (using a staple gun) to the felt-covered side of the board so the shirt is just below the head opening and the sleeves are right by the hand holes. Set the shoes in place below the pant legs.

Make up your assistant's face, add big ears (you can make these out of paper), and have him or her practice acting out the part of the grumpy gremlin, with hands sticking out the armholes and near the end of the gremlin's shirt.

When all is ready, position the little guy in a place where he can have some fun giving everyone who walks by a hard time.

Note: It is best if the board is placed in front of a black background.

28

Foggy Spooks

Imagine you're lost, slogging through a swamp deep in the jungle. Suddenly, out of the thick fog ahead, the face of a hideous monster appears like magic before you, and you know your number's up. But then, just as mysteriously, a breeze arises and the face disappears.

You can create this and other truly bizarre visual effects with a little dry ice, a slide projector, and weird slides. You can even have images of your friends' faces appear and disappear in the magic fog.

NOTE: Strange as it may sound, dry ice can actually burn your skin. Make sure an adult wearing heavy gloves handles the dry ice.

PROPS AND PREPARATION

YOU WILL NEED...

- 2 yards of cheesecloth (from a fabric or grocery store)
- Tub of warm water
- Block of dry ice (available at some grocery stores)
- Heavy gloves for handling the dry ice (important)
- Fan
- Slide projector
- Slides of frightening faces—or of your friends' faces
- Eerie music playing on a tape recorder

HOW TO DO IT...

Shred the cheesecloth to look like a spiderweb, and hang it just above a tub filled with warm water so that it provides a surface against which you can project the slides.

Have an adult place the dry ice in the tub of warm water just before you start your spook show; fog will form above and around the tub.

Place the slide projector some distance away and in front of the cheesecloth. It should project images against the cheesecloth and into the fog.

A fan some distance from the tub, set on low, may help direct the fog up into the cloth. Then, advance the images through the slide projector. Spooky music playing in the background will add nicely to the effect.

HOPPING HAUNTS

This simplest of all tricks has astounded audiences for years. You'll laugh to learn that you can make ghosts dance with only a white handkerchief and some "invisible" black thread.

PROPS AND PREPARATION

YOU WILL NEED...

- ■ *White handkerchief*
- ■ *Black thread*
- ■ *Black material as a backdrop*
- ■ *Hidden assistant*

HOW TO DO IT...

The success of this trick depends on two things. First, you need a backdrop that's dark enough to hide the thread supporting the little ghost. Second, your offstage assistant must do some clever handiwork to cause the spook to dance in a lifelike way by tugging on the thread.

Set the scene by tying a knot in the top of the handkerchief and around a black thread that runs across the length of the room (see illustration).

Your assistant (who can be hiding behind a piece of furniture) should practice the ghost dance ahead of time so the movements of the hanky look believable.

By pulling and loosening the tension on the black thread, the handkerchief can be made to jump up, dance, soar into the air, and fall to the ground.

CROAK!
CROAK!

HISSS!

PROPS AND PREPARATION

YOU WILL NEED...

- *Block of dry ice broken apart into several chunks the size of soup cans (available at some grocery stores)*

- *Heavy gloves for handling the dry ice (important)*

- *3 or 4 pails filled with warm water*

- *Fan*

- *2 dim nightlights with green Christmas lightbulbs*

- *Hidden tape recorder playing spooky swamp sounds*

HOW TO DO IT...

The fog in your bog can be easily created by buying a few pounds of dry ice (that is, ice that's made of frozen carbon dioxide rather than water), which gives off a wonderfully thick fog as it melts in warm water.

You may want to put a small fan near the dry ice to spread the fog around the room. Some spooky swamp sounds played on a tape recorder and the two dim nightlights placed at floor level will add tremendously to the weirdness of your indoor fog bog.

If you live in an area that has crickets chirping at night, take a cassette tape recorder outside and just record the sounds of nature. You may want to add your own noises (howls, screeches, yelps) to the background sound of the crickets for an added effect.

NOTE: *This effect uses dry ice... nasty stuff that is so cold it can actually burn your skin. Make sure an adult wearing heavy gloves handles the dry ice.*

THE FOG BOG

Swamp time again! Your friends will have their share of foggy fits when they wander into a room where the floor is swimming with an eerie colored mist. Play a recording of frogs croaking and snakes hissing, and your terrified companions will be clambering for higher ground.

FAKE FIRE

There's something irresistible about a fire. Stone Age hunters shared stories of courage around a fire on cold winter nights. Campers huddle close to a fire to tell tales of terror. And guests of your haunted house will be drawn like magnets to the well-made illusion of an open fire.

PROPS AND PREPARATION

YOU WILL NEED...

- *Strips of orange or yellow chiffon fabric about 16" long*
- *Scissors*
- *A large can, pot, or tub (a giant-size popcorn tin also works well)*
- *Duct tape*
- *Hairdryer*
- *String of red Christmas lights*

HOW TO DO IT...

Cut or tear the strips of fabric to make them ragged. Build your fake fire by attaching the ragged strips to the edge of the pot, can, or tub, using duct tape.

Place the hairdryer inside the pot and tape it so that it blows upward, causing the chiffon to flutter like flames.

Position the red Christmas lights so they shine up on the chiffon as it flutters. The effect will look like large flames dancing in the pot.

CAUTION: Never leave the pot unattended, and operate the hairdryer only a few minutes at a time so it doesn't overheat.

BLACK THREAD MAGIC

Science has given us video games, skateboards, and the starship *Enterprise*. But those marvelous inventions pale in comparison to that wondrous miracle substance, the all-but-invisible black thread. Never heard of it? Well, when you've seen the dazzling results it produces in your haunted house, you'll never leave home without it. Keep in mind, however, that the black thread's invisibility depends on having a dark enough background behind it so that it blends in.

PROPS AND PREPARATION

WHAT YOU'LL NEED AND HOW IT'S DONE...

■ Doors mysteriously open and close by tying black thread to the doorknob and pulling on it from a hidden place.

■ Shoes belonging to a shuffling "invisible man" can be slid, one after another, by black thread across the floor.

■ Make groping hands by blowing up rubber gloves, tying them off like a balloon, and suspending them from the ceiling by—what else?—black thread.

■ Bring seemingly lifeless rats (fake ones, of course; see page 16) to life and send them skittering across the floor with a tug on an attached length of black thread.

■ With black thread you can mysteriously pull books off a bookshelf from across the room.

■ Plastic jack-o'-lanterns or skulls can be made to float and swing through the room by dangling them from black thread.

FINGER RIPPER

The first job of any magician is to dazzle the crowd with a trick that leaves them in awe. From that point on, they're hungry for more and completely under your (bionic) thumb. Finger Ripper will accomplish this job handily...with a little luck, you may even complete the trick with both hands intact!

YUK!

JOIN COVERED BY FIRST FINGER

THE WAY THEY SEE IT!

THE WAY YOU SEE IT.

PROPS AND PREPARATION

YOU WILL NEED...

■ *2 hands (your own) with fingers fully functional and in place*

HOW TO DO IT...

If you're right-handed, place your right hand in front of you with your palm facing your body and your thumb bent back at a ninety-degree angle (lefties, do everything the opposite way).

Bend the thumb of your left hand as illustrated on this page, place it against the "stump" of your bent right thumb, and cover the "severed" joint with your left index finger.

Then, after visibly psyching yourself up and prepping your audience for an unbelievable feat, "rip" the two parts of your bionic thumb apart and quickly put the pieces back together.

Pretend to be exhausted from this superhuman accomplishment.

Note: To pull this off, practice the trick many times in front of a mirror so that you can see your hands the way an audience will.

NOSE BREAKER

OUCH! SNAP! CRUNCH!

Nose Breaker works well as an alternative to Finger Ripper (see previous page) for proving to your audience that you have been born with a mind-boggling combination of supernatural, mutant, and bionic powers. If your crowd thinks they know you well enough to doubt it, then pull out all the stops and give them both tricks... they'll have no choice but to believe what their eyes tell them is obviously true.

PROPS AND PREPARATION

YOU WILL NEED...

■ *2 hands (the same as those used in the last trick) and the nose on your face*

■ *A hanky (optional)*

HOW TO DO IT...

Announce that your extensive magic training and mutated biology allow you to snap bones and other breakable body parts and then heal them at will. To demonstrate this, you will crunch the joint in your nose and then snap it back into place.

Following the illustration on this page, place both hands in front of your face and pretend to push your nose radically from side to side. Secretly slip a thumbnail behind your upper front teeth and snap it against the teeth in time to your apparently brutal nose adjustments.

After you've miraculously restored your nose to form, and as your friends stare in disbelief, take out a hanky and give the old snooter a blow so they can see the thing still works!

THE MYSTERY GRIP

In this stunt, the simple act of getting a grip on yourself will draw shouts of amazement and fits of laughter from your friends. As you stand before them holding a large cloth in front of you with both of your hands, a third hand suddenly reaches up from behind the cloth and wraps its fingers around your throat, seemingly in a death grip. You stagger and struggle, barely able to talk, before collapsing on the floor.

PROPS AND PREPARATION

YOU WILL NEED...

- *Scarf or piece of cloth about 3' square*
- *A 1/4" to 1/2" wide wooden dowel or stick about 3' long*
- *Safety pins (6)*
- *Pair of stiff gloves that will hold the shape of your hand, even when you take it out of the glove*
- *Household glue*

HOW TO DO IT...

The dowel must be attached to the top edge of the cloth so that it's invisible. Do this by folding a one-inch strip of the cloth over the dowel and securing it in place with the safety pins (see illustration). Then glue one of the gloves to the cloth so it is positioned as if a hand inside it were holding up the cloth.

Put on the unattached glove and slip your hand into the attached glove as you pick up the cloth (you'll need to do this smoothly so people don't see that one glove is glued to the cloth). Standing before your audience, tell them you're going to cause a spirit to appear behind the cloth.

Say that you're feeling nervous about this spirit and that you really need to get a grip on yourself. As you say this, slip your hand free from the attached glove and, while holding up the cloth and attached glove with the other hand, reach up from behind the cloth with your free hand and pretend to choke yourself.

As you collapse to the floor, secretly slip your hand back into the glove.

ATTACHED GLOVE

The Hand Thing

Ever notice that your hand almost has a life of its own? Like the last time it helped itself when you walked by the cookie jar. Or when it couldn't resist pushing all the buttons on your way out the elevator door. Well, that's tame compared to the free spirit your hand becomes in this special effect. Once "detached" from the rest of your body, your hand will be able to dance, communicate in sign language, play the drums...you name it. In fact, the possibilities are only limited by your...er, its...imagination.

PROPS AND PREPARATION

YOU WILL NEED...

- *Cardboard or wooden shoe box (with lid), with the bottom cut off*
- *Poster paint*
- *Wooden board approximately 3' square, with a hole cut in the middle (the hole should be large enough for you to put your hand through)*
- *2 chairs placed back-to-back, with the wooden board on top of them*
- *Black curtains or a black cloth large enough to wrap around the board and chairs so they look like a big, draped table*
- *Thumbtacks*

HOW TO DO IT...

If you're at all handy, you should have no trouble pulling off this startling special effect. First, paint the box according to your tastes. Then thumbtack the black curtain or cloth to the edge of the board so no one can see you—or your trusty assistant—hiding underneath.

Stick your hand through the hole in the board and into the box. Surprise your guests as they walk through your haunted house by popping up and knocking the lid high into the air, or waving to them, when they least expect it.

For added fun, you can show your audience a stuffed glove. As they watch, the glove is placed inside the box, which is then closed. A moment later, the top of the box creeps up, revealing that the magic hand has come to life!

Only you and your assistant know that the stuffed glove drops through the hole in the box, and the real hand wears a duplicate glove.

THE GHOST GALLERY

In the Ghost Gallery, even the walls have eyes. Your guests will do a double take when they notice that some of the portraits hanging innocently about are tracking their every move.

PROPS AND PREPARATION

YOU WILL NEED...

- *Inexpensive poster portrait (available from a poster store, or you can paint your own)*
- *Cardboard backing material sized to fit the poster*
- *Scissors*
- *Glue stick or household glue*
- *Old sheet*
- *Thumbtacks*
- *Picture wire*
- *Duct tape*

HOW TO DO IT...

Using glue or a glue stick, mount the poster onto the cardboard. Carefully cut the eyes out of your poster portrait (and cardboard).

Tack an old sheet to the rafters and hang the poster from picture wire in front of the sheet. Cut a hole in the sheet so your eyes can look through the holes in the poster. It looks eerie to see a flat picture with real human eyes that move.

You can also cut out the full face, and use duct tape on the back of the poster to hinge it so it can open and close like a door.

Your guests will first see the regular picture; then your face can suddenly appear to welcome them to your haunted house, where anything can happen!

DR. JEKYLL'S POTION

Add a couple of drops from the test tube held in your shaking hand, take a sip from the foaming potion, and your friends will slip into deep shock to see what you've become...Oh NO!!...Not him!!...Not that!!!

PROPS AND PREPARATION

YOU WILL NEED...

■ *A clear glass, 1/4 full of green water (use a few drops of food coloring)*

■ *1 teaspoon of baking soda*

■ *Test tube containing 3 tablespoons of vinegar (or you can use another glass)*

■ *Card table covered with an old sheet*

■ *Monster mask*

■ *White laboratory coat (optional)*

■ *Test tubes, beakers, and other laboratory artifacts (optional)*

HOW TO DO IT...

Have the glass of colored water ready beforehand and set it on the table with the vinegar-filled test tube and teaspoon of baking soda. You can set the stage further by setting up beakers, a scale, and other laboratory equipment in the background.

Tell your audience that you have been perfecting a magic potion and that they will witness your first experiment with the mysterious formula. Then mix the baking soda into the glass and stir it. With a shaking hand, add the vinegar. The mixture will start to foam wildly—pretend to take a sip and fall to the floor behind the table, making choking noises and grasping your neck. Quickly, while out of the audience's sight, pull the monster mask on, leap to your feet, and give 'em a frightful roar that will bring down the rafters.

SPIRIT PICTURES

These works of art look normal enough when the lights are on...but hit the dimmer and what was a handsome portrait turns into a sinister glowing skeleton!

PROPS AND PREPARATION

YOU WILL NEED...

- *Inexpensive posters or portraits (available from a poster store at a local mall, or you can paint your own)*
- *Cardboard backing material sized to fit the poster*
- *Glue stick or household glue*
- *Thumbtacks*
- *Picture wire*
- *Green glow-in-the-dark paint that dries clear (available from a theatrical supply store)*

HOW TO DO IT...

Using glue or a glue stick, mount the poster onto the cardboard.

To give your poster portrait that wonderful skeleton look, use the green glow-in-the-dark paint to fashion a skull and skeleton over the portrait. The paint dries almost clear, so the skeleton won't show up until that menacing moment when the lights are turned off.

The effect of seeing what looks like a reproduction of the Mona Lisa turn into a green glowing skeletal creature is truly bizarre!

LIGHTS ON...

LIGHTS OFF..

THE GRABBER

Just when your friends think they're getting a moment's rest from all the horrible happenings in your haunted house, they learn the hard way that even the furniture isn't what it seems to be. Someone sits down in a comfy-looking easy chair in the corner only to discover the chair has a mind...and hands...of its own!

PROPS AND PREPARATION

YOU WILL NEED...

- *An easy chair*
- *A sheet or blanket*

HOW TO DO IT...

This trick is as simple as can be, but the element of surprise will leave your guests gasping for breath. Cover the easy chair with a sheet or blanket that also hides you behind the chair.

When your friend sits down in the chair, suddenly reach around and get a good grip on his or her arms. When the chair shouts "Boo!" as the person is sitting down, watch your victim jump in terror!

COBWEBS

Whether it's the depths of the Mummy's tomb or a haunted cave of lost treasures in the heart of the jungle, have you ever noticed that when it comes to creepy, horrible places, cobwebs seem to be everywhere? And the scarier the place, the bigger the webs?

So to make sure your friends know they're in for the fright of their lives, you'll want the doorways in your haunted house to be thick with giant, dripping monster webs. You can make them feel like they're walking through a cobweb city by following a few simple steps.

PROPS AND PREPARATION

YOU WILL NEED...

- Lightweight string, cut into 4' lengths
- Masking tape
- Bowl of water

HOW TO DO IT...

Tape the string so that it hangs in single strands, spaced about three inches apart, from the top of a doorway.

Dip the ends of the string in a bowl of water before your first guests arrive. As people pass through the dimly lit doorway, it will feel like they just walked into Creepy Hollow.

42

PROPS AND PREPARATION

■ *SEVERED FINGERS?* No cause for panic—it's just a bunch of hot dogs cut in half lengthwise.

■ *VEINS?* Cooked spaghetti noodles with a touch of red and blue food coloring, that's all.

■ *INTESTINES?* Don't bust a gut, it's only pasta noodles with a few chunks of gelatin added for effect.

■ *THOSE BULGING EYEBALLS?* Just an innocent batch of cocktail onions rolling around in a bowl.

A FEW GOOD PARTS

Your uncle has been busy again...you know, the one who was kicked out of medical school. It looks as though he's been dissecting that cadaver he stole from the morgue. And, unfortunately, in the dimly lit basement your friends just stumbled onto several bowls of body parts that he really should have disposed of properly.

Be sure you announce the name of each body part before your friends touch them.

WIND AND CHILLS

Drapes mysteriously moving, shudders flapping against walls, and wind blowing on guests help to set the mood. Houses of horror always seem to be teased and haunted by the wind, and yours should be no exception.

PROPS AND PREPARATION

Creating chilling wind effects involves a careful mix of sounds and mysterious movements and drafts created by well-placed fans. The wind sounds can be soft (see pages 55 to 56 for more information); they will quietly create a spooky mood.

Also, try the following effects using fans:

■ A fan placed so it causes light curtains to blow gently and shimmer will add to the spooky mood.

■ Fans that greet unsuspecting friends with a sudden blast of air can have a startling effect.

■ An oscillating fan (one that turns back and forth) that blows every few moments against the back of a rocking chair can create the illusion that a ghost has settled down to read the evening paper.

Note: For this effect, you may need to attach a piece of cardboard to the back of the rocker so the fan has something solid to blow against. The cardboard acts like a ship's sail.

GETTING BUGGED

Nothing like a teeming horde of carnivorous insects to make the skin of your haunted housemates crawl. Just start talking about creepy critters and most folks will get jumpy. A few tricks with your collection of fake insects and your friends will be bugged all night! So dim the lights and have some fun.

PROPS AND PREPARATION

WHAT YOU'LL NEED AND HOW TO DO IT...

■ *LICE.* A few grains of rice sprinkled in the hair gives the unmistakable impression that nasty little lice-like creatures have found a new home.

■ *WASPS OR JUNE BUGS.* Quietly dropping a few raisins on the back of your friends' necks will cause quite a stir.

■ *WORMS.* Have your guests close their eyes and sink a hand into a bowl of gummy worms (they're even more unpleasant with a little water sprinkled on them). These slimy critters will be the life of the party.

■ *NIGHT CRAWLERS.* A nice bowl or two of cooked macaroni will round out any meal (and your parents are concerned you're not eating right?).

■ *CATERPILLARS.* Ask your parents if they can spare a foot or two of cotton clothesline. Cut it into two-inch lengths, turn down the lights, and you've got yourself a minicaterpillar convention.

■ *COCKROACHES.* As your guests pass through the darkened room, tell them to be careful not to step on the cockroaches because they "squish" when stepped on. Don't tell them that you've sprinkled a few peanut shells around the floor; your guests will swear the place is alive with crunchy, creepy crawlers.

45

WALKING ON BONES

A friendly mouse or a cozy nest of termites are the only uninvited guests found in most houses. But, as you explain to your guests, your haunted house is positively creeping with creatures of all kinds, both living and dead. Skeletons are stacked in every closet and bones just seem to show up everywhere. (To make the point, quickly open and close a closet door to reveal a paper skeleton hanging inside and reach between couch cushions to pull up a hefty bone.) Tell your visitors they'd better watch their step; there's no telling whose bones they're likely to find underfoot.

PROPS AND PREPARATION

YOU WILL NEED...

- *Dry bread (5 or 6 slices)*
- *Big pretzel sticks (5 or 6)*
- *Old rug*
- *Paper skeleton*
- *Large bone (available from a butcher shop)*

HOW TO DO IT...

Dry the bread by letting it sit out for several days or, with an adult's help, bake it in an oven at a low temperature. Distribute the bread underneath the old rug and put it in places where the light is dim so the bumps aren't noticeable.

Add a few pretzel sticks for added bone-crunching fun. After setting up the trick as described above, lead your guests across the rug and tell that what a boneyard your house has become!

WHAT A BRAIN!

Your friends might not have known that brain surgery was one of your favorite pastimes, but just tell them you've always been a little shy. Then lead them into your operating room...which must be kept dimly lit in order to preserve your specimens...and ask if they'd like to meet one of the best brains in the business. As they step forward to make their acquaintances with your brain of all brains, you'd better brace yourself for some head-splitting screams.

PROPS AND PREPARATION

YOU WILL NEED...

- *Red or pink medium-sized round balloon*
- *Warm water*
- *Small dish (like a pie plate)*
- *Strawberry jam*

HOW TO DO IT...

Fill the balloon with water so it's about the size of a softball, tie the end, and place it on the plate. Coat the outside of the balloon with strawberry jam.

Invite your victims to touch the slimy blob of cells on the plate (the warm water in the balloon will make the brain feel like it was just popped out of a skull).

Remember to tell everyone to touch and not pick up the brain. If they want to play brain toss, let them use their own gray matter.

LOOK ALIVE!

The three zombies standing like corpses in their upright coffins just happen to have been struck dead by lightning during a full moon on Halloween. And, as you explain to your wide-eyed guests, that means anyone who touches all three of these gruesome stiffs with his or her eyes closed is guaranteed a year's worth of good luck.

The trick? When your brave guests step forward to go toe-to-toe with these hideous creatures, one of them suddenly comes to life and, with a menacing growl, begins to quiver from the victim's touch. How's that for good luck?

PROPS AND PREPARATION

YOU WILL NEED...

- 3 coffins (see page 20)
- 2 stuffed dummies (see page 22) with zombie masks
- Costume for your assistant that matches the ones on the two dummy zombies
- Zombie Makeup

HOW TO DO IT...

Keep the lights dimmed and the live zombie still. The fun comes as the guest reaches out to touch the zombies. Just remember, never have your zombie grab the victim.... It's okay to frighten them a little, but don't terrorize anyone.

MYSTERY BOX

PROPS AND PREPARATION

YOU WILL NEED...

- *Several cardboard shoe boxes*
- *Poster paints*
- *Tape*
- *Cotton*
- *Shaving cream*
- *Hunks of fake fur (from a costume or fabric store)*
- *Wet towel*
- *A tape recorder playing bee sounds and growling sounds*
- *A piece of plywood with a hand-size hole cut in the middle*
- *Two sawhorses*
- *An old bed sheet*

HOW TO DO IT...

Prepare your mystery boxes by cutting in the top of each shoe box a hole that's just big enough to fit a hand. Put the materials inside (see below) and tape the boxes shut. Then paint the boxes black, and write scary-sounding clues about what might be inside on signs near the boxes.

- **HORNET'S NEST.** Your friends will be buzzing when they feel the cotton balled up inside this box and hear your hidden tape recorder playing bee sounds.

- **RABID CRITTER.** A few hunks of fake fur will come to life when the tape recorder lets out a frightful growl.

- **MYSTERY GOO.** When your friends discover a pile of shaving cream in this box, they'll think they've been slimed by a ghost or an alien.

- **SURPRISE!** The scariest mystery of all is the simplest: Make an extra hand-sized hole in the bottom of this box. Make a hole in the top of a wooden board set on top of two sawhorses that are covered with a bed sheet. Hide an assistant underneath this fake table with his hand through the hole. As your guests' hands reach in to explore the wet towel, the live hand hiding beneath it suddenly comes to life.

The ultimate touchy-feely test for the bravest visitors of your haunted house is the Mystery Box. Who can be sure what lurks inside this series of closed boxes, each with a hand-sized opening that invites the curious to see what mysteries they will uncover.

(Caution: Don't put anything sharp or in any way dangerous inside the mystery boxes.)

SINISTER SMELLS

If you've ever had the distinct pleasure of wading through a swamp or petting a dog who's been playing with a skunk, you know how powerful your sense of smell can be. Put it to use in your house of horrors to work sinister magic on your guests. The effect will be especially powerful if offensive orders are used creatively in a dimly lit room with objects that are touched and smelled.

WEREWOLF BLOOD

DECOMPOSING DIGITS

WHAT YOU'LL NEED AND HOW TO DO IT...

■ *DECOMPOSING DIGITS.* Have some stinky limburger cheese handy when your guests explore the bowl of "severed fingers" that seem to be rotting (see page 43).

■ *FUNERAL FLOWERS.* Strongly scented flowers or floral room deodorant near any coffins you have lying about suggest the smell of a funeral parlor.

■ *GARLIC NECKLACES.* String a few cloves of garlic together to spook vampires. Your friends may feel more secure wearing garlic necklaces, too.

■ *WEREWOLF BLOOD.* Nothing more than a cup of vinegar. Let your guests take a whiff and even have them stick their fingers in the cup to taste...yuck!

■ *CREATURE PERSPIRATION.* Place a cut onion under an old T-shirt and let your guests smell the shirt of a creature that needs a lesson in personal hygiene.

■ *PHANTOM ASHES.* A jar filled with pepper has a wicked, bitter smell... Achoo!

■ *MUMMY BREATH.* Liquid smoke (available from a grocery store) has an odor like a 2,000-year-old mummy. Appetizing, huh?

■ *WITCH'S POTIONS.* Various strong-scented herbs and spices such as rosemary, caraway, thyme, and cloves can be placed in small jars or cups labeled with stickers that say things like... bat toenails, lizard scales, turtle tongues, fish scales, and crispy crickets.

A BONEYARD BASH

What home is complete without a few seedy ancestors pushing up daisies in the back yard? Or make that the front yard...no shame in the fact that Great-Uncle Fred died with an ax in his head, or that "sweet" Cousin Nell now resides in...well, you get the idea.

Design your cemetery well and it may become a sinister sensation on your block...if not the talk of the entire terrified town. Of course, you'll need to get a parental stamp of approval, since creating a boneyard in your front yard probably means altering the normal appearance of the house (if it doesn't, you have no need for this book!).

To set the proper mood, you'll want to display a good collection of gravestones sticking up out of the ground at odd angles (page 21) and perhaps a couple of dead dummies lying about waiting their turn to be laid under (page 22). If your parents don't object, a partially dug grave with a pile of dirt and a couple of shovels beside it is a great reminder to visitors that their time is yet to come! Also, be sure to light the cemetery at night with flashlights or flood-lights that are bright enough so everyone can read who's lying six feet under each marker.

51

EPITAPHS

Create your own clever epitaphs (written messages) for your gravestones, or use some of these:

RECORDING GHOSTLY SOUNDS

The wind begins to moan
The light's gone out,
And rats are scampering
Roundabout.
Screams in the morning,
Howls at night,
These, yes, these, are the sounds of fright!!

You've heard them...those strange noises outside your window that wake you from a dead sleep, the mysterious footsteps in the hall that cause you to hold your breath so tight you can hear the pounding of your own terrified heart. Well, you'll want to provide the same spooky sounds that will cause your haunted housemates to shiver in terror.

The easiest way to get your hands on great sound effects is to see if your local public library has any recordings of spooky sounds. You may find sound effect records, tapes, and CDs with everything from scratching rodents and creaking gates to screaming witches and pounding rainstorms.

It's also fun and easy to record your own ghastly sound effects on a cassette tape recorder. One option is to actually record the real sounds themselves...this works well for sounds that you can easily capture without doing things like breaking windows or standing in front of a galloping horse. Otherwise, you can make your own sound effects by arming yourself with a tape recorder, blank tape, microphone (many tape recorders have built-in microphones), a quiet place to serve as your recording studio, and the right props to get the job done.

SOUND EFFECTS

Here are a few fun ways to use house-hold props to create some startling sound effects that you can capture on your cassette recorder.

CLOMP! RUMBLE!

EEEK!

RATTLE! RATTLE! RATTLE! RATTLE! RATTLE!

RICE

SNAP!

FLAP! FLAP! FLAP!

PROPS AND PREPARATION

WHAT YOU'LL NEED AND HOW TO DO IT...

■ *THUNDER.* Thunder can be recorded live or created by taping the sound of a very large sheet of poster board or, better yet, sheet metal (available from a hardware store) shaken so that it wiggles and wobbles.

■ *RAIN.* You may be able to get the sound of real rain lashing a window. Otherwise, record the sound of rice (uncooked) being poured onto a metal cookie sheet.

■ *FOOTSTEPS.* If you have a room with a slight echo and wooden floors, simply hold the microphone close to the floor as you walk along in a pair of leather shoes. Otherwise, try walking on a wooden board wearing leather shoes.

■ *WOLF HOWLS.* Really nothing to it: Cup your hands around your mouth and let loose with a high-pitched yelping howl. Try it...it's fun!

■ *ROARING FIRE.* Simply crinkle a handful of cellophane or thin plastic wrapping material close to the microphone. A plastic sheet protector also works great.

■ *SCREAMS.* Nothing will do like the real thing. Get several of your friends and, all together, let loose!

■ *BREAKING BONES.* Try snapping carrots in half.

■ *FLAPPING BATS.* Wiggle a plastic bag that has been folded in half in front of the microphone.

MORE SOUND EFFECTS

PROPS AND PREPARATION

WHAT YOU'LL NEED AND HOW TO DO IT...

■ **SLIMY BOG.** You can create this lovely sound by slowly blowing bubbles into a large bowl or tub of water...the slower you blow, the murkier the bog will sound.

■ **SHATTERING GLASS.** No, this is not one you want to try to capture live. Instead get some small pieces of scrap sheet metal from a hardware store and drop them against a cement floor or onto a metal cookie sheet. Crash!

■ **WICKED WIND.** Howling, moaning, wind sounds are a haunted house must! Make them by experimenting with your own voice and by blowing hard into the microphone.

■ **RATTLING CHAINS AND MOANS.** Any cellar dungeon would be incomplete without the racket made by moaning prisoners rattling their chains and banging tin cups against the bars. A heavy bicycle security chain, tin cup, and frying pan are all you need.

■ **CREAKING HINGES.** Hunt around your house or neighborhood until you find a door or gate that's well rusted. Try holding the microphone close to the hinge so the sound reverberates.

■ **MISCELLANEOUS MAYHEM.** Other sounds you can make with your own voice and a few simple objects include: pounding on doors and shouting, a door knocker, muffled shouting, a door slamming shut, chalk screeching on a blackboard, and various moans, groans, shrieks, hollers, and shouts.

Spooky Music

Some music just seems like it was custom-made for haunted houses. A lot of organ music falls into this category. Then there's the music that actually was written for dreary, frightful occasions...like funerals, demented television shows and movies, or just those terrifying moments that life sometimes hands out at no extra charge.

The choice is yours, of course, but when selecting music for your domicile of doom you will never go wrong with the likes of these:

- ■ "The Funeral March of a Marionette" Alfred Hitchcock's theme song
- ■ *The Twilight Zone* television show theme song
- ■ The overture from *The Phantom of the Opera*
- ■ "The Death March," by Chopin
- ■ The soundtrack from the movie *Psycho*
- ■ "The Firebird" by Stravinsky
- ■ "Night on Bald Mountain" by Mussorgsky
- ■ "Toccata and Fugue in D Minor" by Bach

THE FRIGHTFUL POWER OF LIGHT

*Dark devours light
As the day becomes the night,
And the beastly, frightful creatures
Come from shadows back to life!*

Ever notice how the shadows grow long and strange as the sun slips down the sky? And when the moon comes up, the world is bathed in eerie silver light? What a difference light can make! It can change a scene completely, from one that's comfortable and familiar to something sinister and scary.

PROPS AND PREPARATION

Learning to master the use of light in your haunted house puts the very tools of terror in your hands. You don't need to do anything fancy or expensive.

While some of the plans in this chapter call for special lights, you can do wonders with the clever use of a simple flashlight or by placing a little colored gel over a light already in your house.

No matter what kind of lighting you create, however, always remember these things:

■ Never plunge your guests into complete darkness...it's no fun, and someone could easily get hurt. Giving flashlights to everyone who enters your dimly lit haunted house is a great way to help them to safely explore and discover, by themselves, the surprises that await them.

■ Have exit doors and pathways clearly marked, even in dim light. Glow-in-the-dark tape (available from a paint, hobby, theatrical supply, or hardware store) and night lights are good ways to mark exits and guide your friends about when the lights are low. You should keep a light shining on a sign that says EXIT in every room of your haunted house.

■ When working with electrical lights, beware of fire and electrical dangers. Do not place any objects or clothing near light bulbs, and keep all lights and electrical appliances away from water.

LIGHTING EFFECTS

You don't have to be a fat-cat, cigar-smokin' Hollywood producer to make terrific use of special lights to control the mood and feeling of your haunted house, the way it's done in movies and on television. Without spending much money, you can get a few of these same special lights yourself, and work wonders on your little house of horrors.

PROPS AND PREPARATION

YOU WILL NEED...

■ *Black light bulbs (from a theatrical supply store or a store that sells lighting fixtures)*

■ *Strobe lights*

■ *Flicker-flame light bulbs (from a hardware store or a store that sells lighting fixtures)*

■ *Colored light bulbs*

■ *Colored plastic lighting "gel" (from a theatrical supply store)*

HOW TO DO IT...

Black lights (fluorescent lightbulbs that emit ultraviolet light) will make your haunted house-mates look as if they've entered an alien solar system. The whites of their eyes and teeth will shine unnaturally bright, their skin will darken, and any white or brightly colored clothes or objects will give off an unearthly glow.

Objects painted with fluorescent colors will glow so wildly, you'd swear they're radioactive. Black light bulbs will fit most fluorescent light fixtures.

Strobe lights, which photographers use to flash bright white light onto dark scenes, can have great startling effects on your guests...especially if they don't expect it. Be sure not to flash a strobe light directly into your guests' faces. You can use strobe lights to create the effect of lightning, too.

Years ago, rings of lights hanging from ceilings, called chandeliers, were lit by candles. Today, you can buy special candelabra flicker-flame light bulbs that simulate the light of candles. They can be used in your haunted house wherever candlelight would create the perfect mood.

Colored light bulbs screwed into regular lamps can completely change the feeling of a room. You can also buy the same colored plastic lighting "gel" that lighting experts use to color lights for stage productions.

Many of these gels have the additional advantage of being fireproof.

Note: Strobe lights can trigger epileptic seizures.

MONSTER FACES

A single light in a dimly lit room has a way of attracting everyone's attention. Imagine your friends' fright when, with a simple flashlight, all eyes are on you as you transform your friendly face into a that of a menacing monster.

PROPS AND PREPARATION

YOU WILL NEED...

- Flashlight
- Colored lighting gel (from a theatrical supply store)
- Colored transparent plastic cover
- Monster mask
- Plastic light sticks

HOW TO DO IT...

Holding the flashlight at your chin and shining it up into your face creates such weird shadows that you will be nearly unrecognizable. Put on an ugly grin, let out a bloodcurdling laugh, and you'll have everyone wondering what's happening to you.

Try putting some colored lighting gel or a colored transparent plastic cover over the end of a flashlight for an even more sinister look.

Here's a variation on this idea. While no one is looking, put a monster mask on your head backward so it covers the back of your head.

Turn the flashlight on under your chin for a moment, start breathing heavily, and tell everyone that you're suddenly feeling strange. Then turn out the light and unleash a monster-like growl as you spin the mask around to cover your face.

Turn on the light again, this time illuminating your unsightly features. Do this one quickly enough and everyone will be convinced you've transformed yourself into a frightful beast.

Another terrific trick is to get a couple of plastic light sticks that glow like fireflies for about three hours after you've opened them, and then stuff them under your shirt and in the legs of your pants.

The sticks will cause you to cast an eerie glow wherever you go in a darkened room. Tell your guests that you are the victim of a nuclear accident. What a way to glow!

GLOWING PHANTOMS

YOU WILL NEED...

- *Glow-in-the-dark tape and paint (from a theatrical supply or hardware store)*

- *Heavy paper and marking pens for signs*

- *Cold cream or makeup remover*

HOW TO DO IT...

Give everyone a fright by painting ghosts, goblins, or sinister, glowing eyes on sheets of black construction paper and placing them so they stare out from dark corners and closets.

You can also use these radioactive-looking materials to create signs around the house with messages like: "Go Back: Entering Toxic Waste Dump," "Danger: Radioactive Spooks Ahead," or "Mutant Colony: Enter at Your Own Risk."

For a ghoulish guided tour of your haunted house, tape glowing footprints on the floor to guide your guests along.

Use strips of glow-in-the-dark tape, applied to your face in small pieces, to make eyebrows, a nose, mouth, and ears that will glow in the dark as you move around. Do not put the tape on your eyelids... Ouch!

Those same strips of tape on your fingers will make them look like skeleton bones! To remove the tape without also removing your flesh, use some cold cream or makeup remover. Everyone is sure to tell you that your skin has that fresh, healthy glow!

Who knows why, but dark corners and closets have a way of attracting creepy creatures from the spirit realm. Sometimes they're a little hard to see, though. You can help distinguish their features with the creative use of a little glow-in-the-dark tape and paint.

Turn out the lights and this incredible stuff glows like a full moon. Use your imagination and you'll come up with lots of great uses for these wonderful materials.

THE BLACK HOLE

This spooky idea comes to you direct from the depths of outer space, where scientists have found evidence of incredible objects called black holes. These gigantic collapsed stars are so dense and have such strong gravity that everything close by, including the light from nearby stars, gets sucked into them, apparently never to get out.

Believe it or not, making a black hole in your haunted house is simple. And having people and objects magically appear and disappear inside it can be great fun.

PROPS AND PREPARATION

YOU WILL NEED...

■ *A large cardboard box (the type washers or dryers are shipped in)*

■ *Enough black cloth (non-shiny cloth like felt or velour works best) to cover the inside of the box, with a few big scraps left over to make arm sleeves, gloves, and drapes for your props*

■ *Glue*

■ *A roll of black duct tape*

■ *Scissors*

■ *Black poster paint*

■ *A string of Christmas tree lights (white or clear bulbs are best)*

■ *An extension cord*

■ *A pair of white gloves*

■ *A black long-sleeved shirt made from the same material used inside the box*

■ *A pair of black gloves made from the same material*

■ *Various light-colored props that you can make appear and vanish inside the black hole*

HOW TO DO IT...

Prepare the box by sealing the top flaps with duct tape. Cut an opening in the front of the box with scissors (get some help from an adult).

Paint the entire box black, inside and out.

When the paint is dry, carefully cover the inside of the box with the black fabric, attaching it with glue or duct tape.

Cut two arm holes, six to eight inches across, in the middle of the back of the box.

Next attach the Christmas tree lights to the front of the box (the bulbs should not shine inside). When these lights are turned on in a dark room, it will be difficult for anyone to tell how deep the inside of the box is, and that will help you accomplish your effect.

You will also need to make two gloves and two long sleeves that cover the hands and arms of the operator of the black hole. It is best if you can have someone sew a simple long-sleeved shirt out of the same type of fabric that you used to line the inside of the box, and also make a simple pair of gloves or mittens out of the remaining scraps of fabric.

By poking covered arms through the back of the box, your assistant will be invisible to people standing in front of the lights. By covering up light-colored (white and yellow) objects with pieces of black fabric, you can make them disappear. Quickly uncover the same objects, and they will seem to appear from nowhere inside the box.

If your hidden assistant picks up any light-colored object from behind, it will appear to float freely inside the black hole.

Some objects that you may wish to make appear, vanish, or float inside the black hole include:

■ *A plastic pumpkin*

■ *A plastic skull*

■ *A fake head (a mask pulled over a plastic foam wig block)*

■ *A tambourine (that a ghost must be shaking!)*

■ *A bell (that another spirit rings)*

...many other objects could be made to mysteriously move in this amazing chamber.

Another great effect is to have your hidden assistant wear white gloves over his hands. That way, only the hands will be seen moving about the inside of the black hole, with no body attached! It looks very spooky indeed.

When presenting this effect to your friends, have them stand six to eight feet from the front of the box. If they are too close, the illusion does not look as good. Also, keep all the lights off in the room except the Christmas tree lights. Spooky music or sound effects will also add to the effectiveness of the illusion.

LIGHTNING

Lightning managed to bring Frankenstein's monster to life, but it's just as likely to give your guests a heart attack. A blistering crack of simulated lightning at the window and they'll be positively thunderstruck...helped, of course, by an accompanying blast of rolling thunder played on your hidden cassette tape recorder.

PROPS AND PREPARATION

YOU WILL NEED...

- *A sheet of heavy black poster board the size of your window*
- *Tape*
- *Scissors*
- *Camera with a strobe light or flash attached*
- *Cassette tape recorder with a recording of thunder*
- *Wood to make fake window frame (optional)*

HOW TO DO IT...

Fit poster board to the shape of your window or frame the cardboard with wood to make a fake window.

Cut a lightning bolt in the middle of the poster board and tape it to the window. Place the camera strobe light outside the window so its flash fills the opening in the poster board.

Set the strobe so your assistant can cause it to flash and also operate the tape recorder with its thunderous recording at the same time.

63

LIGHTING THE HOUSE

Dracula liked big drippy candles. The Werewolf got all excited whenever the moon was full. And apparently the Mummy was happiest in the complete darkness of his dreary old tomb.

Like these characters, you have some choices when it comes to a lighting plan for your haunted house. Whether you're a fan of doom and gloom, flashing lightning, or the eerie light of the moon above, you want to be sure that the light creates the effect you want, but also that there's enough light to make the place safe.

PROPS AND PREPARATION

WHAT YOU'LL NEED AND HOW TO DO IT...

■ *LUMINARIAS.* A simple way to create a weird atmosphere for a sidewalk or outdoor patio area is to put small Christmas lights inside paper bags anchored to the ground with sand in the bottom. Cut out jack-o'-lantern faces on each bag to light up the pathway to your haunted house. Keep extension cords out of the way so no one trips over them.

■ *GLOW STICKS.* These little glowing bits of plastic tubing (available from a toy store) give off a wonderfully spooky colored glow. Give one to each of your guests to safely light their way throughout your haunted house.

■ *PATIO LIGHTS WITH GEL.* A little lighting gel...the special colored plastic used at theaters for coloring lights...can do wonders for creating spooky effects with patio lamps. Consider wrapping all the lights outside your home with green lighting gel for a truly eerie effect.

■ *JACK-O'-LANTERNS.* Not only do the good old jack-o'-lanterns give off frightful light, they're also great fun to make. Never place a lit candle inside the pumpkin unless it is to be used outside, and then only if an adult says it is okay.

LIGHTING TEMPLATES

To magically transform the following templates into spooky shadows on the walls or floor of your haunted house, follow these simple steps.

PROPS AND PREPARATION

YOU WILL NEED...

- *Access to a photocopy machine*
- *Glue*
- *Light cardboard*
- *Scissors*
- *Lamp or other light fixture*
- *Large white bed sheet*
- *Duct tape*

HOW TO DO IT...

Photocopy the templates (they can also be enlarged). Glue the photocopy to a piece of light cardboard (like that from a box of cereal or potato chips).

Cut the cardboard, following the outline of the template. Place a light fixture or lamp behind the cardboard template or stencil. Be careful to keep the template from touching the bulb.

Move the template until it casts the shadow where you want it. Try to hide the lamp so that only the shadow is seen. It looks great if you set this up behind a large white bed sheet that has been attached to the ceiling with duct tape.

You may want to flash the light on or off a couple of times to make the ghostly shadows appear and disappear or have shadows cast on window shades or drapes from inside the house.

65

Spooky Hand

See page 65 for directions.

Mr. Ribs

See page 65 for directions.

EERIE EYES

See page 65 for directions.

BOOGIE MAN

See page 65 for directions.

WEIRD WITCH

See page 65 for directions.

SPINNING SPIDER

See page 65 for directions.

BLOOD FORMULA

The sight of blood...in some cases the mere mention of the word...is enough to cause some people to faint. So you won't need much of this stuff in your haunted house. A dash here, a splatter there, and your friends will be bloody scared, indeed!

Keep in mind when you make and use fake blood that, besides looking horrible, the following mixture will stain clothes, carpets, and any other cloth furnishings.

PROPS AND PREPARATION

YOU WILL NEED...

- *Corn syrup (1 cup; Karo brand works great)*
- *Red food coloring (1 teaspoon)*
- *A little water for thinning the mixture*
- *Container with a lid that can be used for storage*

HOW TO DO IT...

Just mix the ingredients listed above into a small bowl, using a few drops of water to achieve the consistency that you want.

Apply the blood sparingly to old shirts, bandages, and whatever body parts need that wonderful bloody look. Store the mixture in a sealed container.

> Note: Food coloring can stain fabric, furniture and carpets. Use only with old clothes.

BLOOD BOMBS

Of course, for some folks...particularly the hardened criminal types...sprinkling blood all over yourself and about the place won't even cause them to bat an eye. For this crowd, you may need to resort to more drastic measures. The Blood Bomb is sure to do the trick.

PROPS AND PREPARATION

YOU WILL NEED...

■ *Small round balloons*

■ *Mixture of fake blood (see previous page)*

■ *Paper towels*

■ *Safety pins or adhesive tape*

■ *Old, light-colored shirt (make sure you use an old shirt since the fake blood will stain it)*

HOW TO DO IT...

Fill a balloon with a few tablespoons of fake blood. The round part of the balloon is full but the neck is empty. Leave the balloons untied and wipe off any excess blood mixture from the outside.

Tape or pin the balloon(s) with the neck pointing up (so the blood won't come out until you're ready) to the inside of your shirt.

Pretending that you've just been smacked by an invisible monster, or hit by an unidentified projectile, slap your shirt where the balloon is hidden, and force the fake blood to spurt out.

Then, when you've made a bloody mess of yourself (being careful not to stain the carpet), you may act out a gruesome, writhing death before your truly shocked friends.

THEY GOT ME!

73

ROTTING FLESH

If you've ever known any spooks that have been dead for a long time...mummies, ghouls, zombies, vampires, and the like...you probably noticed their problem with rotting flesh. After several hundred years, even the best complexions just can't seem to hold up.

And when your friends see the amazing effects created by a little oatmeal and water on your skin, they'll spend the rest of the night trying to figure out in which century and castle you were born!

PROPS AND PREPARATION

YOU WILL NEED...

- *Dry oatmeal (1 1/2 cups)*
- *Water (1/4 cup)*
- *Red food coloring*
- *Mixing bowl*

HOW TO DO IT...

Mix the oatmeal and water in the mixing bowl until it's a thick paste. Apply a little of the oatmeal paste to your cheeks and arms.

Apply layers of the paste in an oval shape with an open middle (like a flat donut) to create the effect of an open wound on your arm. Now apply a few drops of red food coloring to the middle of the wound.

After a while, the mixture will begin to dry out and flake off...when that happens, you'll really be showing your age!

(Remember, only apply the food coloring to the oatmeal and not to your skin, since it can stain.)

POPPED EYEBALLS

Just looking around at the gruesome and bizarre exhibits in your haunted house is likely to cause your guests to adopt the drop-jawed, pop-eyed look. You know, that open-mouth, drooling, dead stare, eyes-bulging-from-their-sockets look that's so popular with zombies? Well, here's a recipe for taking this fearsome fashion statement one ugly step further.

YOU WILL NEED...

- ■ *Marshmallows (2)*
- ■ *Green olive*
- ■ *Dinner knife (ask an adult to help you)*
- ■ *Black makeup or dark eye shadow*

HOW TO DO IT...

First, roll each of the marshmallows in your hands to make them round like eyeballs. To make the irises, use the dinner knife to slice the olive in half.

Make a hole in each marshmallow with your finger and insert the olive half so that part of it sticks out from the marshmallow.

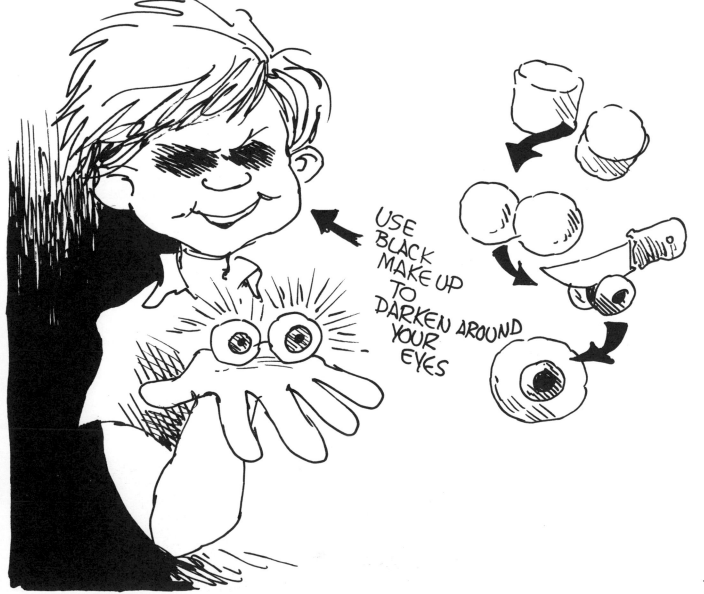

USE BLACK MAKE UP TO DARKEN AROUND YOUR EYES

DELICIOUS DIRT

Ever wonder what the creatures of the night eat during the hundreds and thousands of years that they're packed away in some dark and dingy grave? One look at their dirt-smeared faces as they rise from their graves should give you a clue.

This recipe for Delicious Dirt not only looks great plastered on your zombie face, it actually tastes terrific...especially with a few gummy worms thrown in.

PROPS AND PREPARATION

YOU WILL NEED...

- *Package of Oreo™ or Hydrox™ cookies*
- *Small mixing bowl*
- *A little water*
- *Some gummy worms*

HOW TO DO IT...

Take each cookie apart and remove the white filling (discard or eat it—some spooks find this stuff tasty).

Crush the cookies (filling removed) in a bowl and mix in a few drops of water until the concoction looks like dirt. If you add more water to the mixture, it will look like mud.

Use the Delicious Dirt to cover the lower part of your face (keep it out of your eyes) and your hands.

You can play the generous ghost host and offer some Delicious Dirt to your friends when they arrive at your haunted house. Have a bowl of dirt with some gummy worms on top as a welcome appetizer.

YUM! YUM!

GO AHEAD! TAKE A BITE!

GREEN OOZE

For many of your haunted house guests, the Delicious Dirt trick (see the previous page) will be just about enough to turn their stomachs inside out. But in every crowd there always seems to be one or two characters with guts made of stone...or is it stainless steel? For them, you can always resort to popping a neck vein and spraying a lethal dose of Green Ooze. Gross is good!

PROPS AND PREPARATION

YOU WILL NEED...

- *Guacamole mix (available at grocery stores)*
- *Mixing bowl*
- *Small pitcher of water*
- *Rubber ear syringes (2) (available from a drug store)*
- *(2) 2' lengths of flexible rubber or plastic tubing (aquarium air pump tubing from a pet supply store works great)*
- *Adhesive tape*
- *Old shirt*
- *Newspapers*

HOW TO DO IT...

Guacamole—a wonderful lime-green, creamy Mexican dip made from avocados—has some great properties. For one thing, it's delicious. Even better, it looks completely disgusting when it appears to shoot out, zombie-style, from the veins in your neck.

Prepare the guacamole mix in the bowl according to the directions on the package. Don't worry about the taste, how the stuff looks is more important. Add water to the mixture until it is runny like a cream soup.

Dip the end of each ear syringe into the mixture, and suck up as much ooze as you can into the bulb. Push the ends of the plastic tubing over the end of both syringes (the tubing should fit snugly) and squeeze enough into the tubes until they are full.

You may have to refill the ear syringe with guacamole several times to get fluid all the way through the tube.

Carefully place syringes under each arm and hold them in place with adhesive tape. Put on an old shirt, and carefully bring the tubes up your back so the end of the tubes appear just under the inside collar of your shirt.

Hold these ends in position with adhesive tape. Cover the floor with newspapers so you don't get ooze all over.

EAR SYRINGE

AQUARIUM AIR PUMP TUBING...2 FEET

TAPE

AND...

GUACAMOLE

When it's time to perform, tell your friends that you have been feeling ill lately...as if the veins in your neck are about to burst. As you say this, squeeze your arms against your body and shoot the green ooze out of the top of your shirt collar.

Let the ooze cover your shirt and drip down on the newspaper-covered floor (please don't try this on carpeting). Be very careful not to apply too much pressure and ooze on anyone else's clothes, unless you want to see your guests turn into monsters!

FAKE SCARS AND ROTTEN TEETH

Being in the haunted-house business provides a great excuse to transform yourself into the creatures that live only in your imagination. And a terrific tool for changing yourself into ghouls, goblins, and ghosts is a special kind of wax used by actors, called derma wax. Using this stuff, along with some other simple makeup techniques, lets you bring the creatures of your imagination to life with some truly awesome effects.

PROPS AND PREPARATION

YOU WILL NEED...

- *Derma wax (from a costume or theatrical supply store)*
- *Orange*
- *Dinner knife (ask an adult to help you)*

HOW TO DO IT...

With a little practice you'll be able to use the flesh-colored derma wax to make almost anything, from an enlarged nose to fake ears, scars, and severed fingers or toes. It will take you down whatever haunted path your imagination leads.

The wax softens easily from the warmth of your hand, and it can be shaped around your nose or ears to enlarge them or make them pointed.

Even without derma wax, you can create some fun makeup effects using objects likely to be found in your house.

Begin by cutting an orange into four equal pieces and removing the wedge-shaped peel from one. Turn the section of the peel inside out and use the knife to cut a row of upper and lower big and ugly teeth.

Insert the peel in your mouth behind your lips and the realistic-looking monster's teeth will startle you—not to mention your friends.

PEEL BACK

CUT TEETH

ORANGE

THE INVISIBLE MAN AND HIS DOG

PROPS AND PREPARATION

YOU WILL NEED...

- *An old suit, shirt, tie, socks and shoes*
- *Bathroom tissue*
- *White adhesive tape*
- *Sunglasses*
- *Hat and gloves*
- *About 6' of cotton clothesline with a hollow core (remove the strings running through the middle of the clothesline)*
- *Wire coat hanger, carefully unwound and straightened*

HOW TO DO IT...

Announce to your guests that an invisible man and his dog are present in the room. If they don't believe you, ask them to prove you're wrong.

As they're thinking that one over, ask the invisible man to put some clothes on so they can see him. Tell your guests that the invisible man will be back in a minute.

In a few moments, the invisible man makes his dramatic entrance into the room wearing an old suit, hat, gloves, sunglasses, and bathroom tissue carefully wrapped mummy-style around his face and hair (use adhesive tape to secure the tissue, and don't wrap too tightly around the mouth and nose).

Your friends will know the invisible man's dog is there too, because they will see the leash straining as he pulls.

Create the leash effect by inserting a coat hanger into the hollow clothesline and make a round loop at the end as if the rope were around the dog's neck.

Tie a loop at the other end to hold onto and bend the leash naturally. Practice wiggling the leash as if an invisible dog were tugging it!

What fun it would be to be invisible! How incredible it would be to be able to drift through space, going where you want and doing what you want without the people around you having a clue as to what you're up to. Try this special costume effect and you'll get a taste of what life might be like for such a marvelous person...and an invisible dog.

A Big Hairy Ape

Invite a Big Hairy Ape to your haunted happening, and he's guaranteed to steal the show. Any creature that can climb to the top of a skyscraper and swat airplanes with his bare hands will definitely increase the excitement level a few notches. Here's how you can put the hairy ape together.

PROPS AND PREPARATION

YOU WILL NEED...

- *Fake black fur (5 or 6 yards, from a fabric store)*
- *Scissors*
- *Large coveralls with long sleeves*
- *An adult (to do the sewing) and sewing machine*
- *Heavy black thread*
- *Black gloves*
- *Old black shoes*
- *Hot glue gun (have an adult help you with this)*
- *Black spray paint*
- *Old mask*
- *Toy airplanes (2)*

HOW TO DO IT...

Bringing a Big Hairy Ape to life involves quite a bit of simple sewing, but the result will last for years and can be used by kids of various sizes and even adults.

Cut the fake fur into strips that fit large areas of the coveralls and pin them in place. Then, one by one, sew the fur strips onto the coveralls.

You don't have to worry about doing the seams carefully, since the thick fur will cover them up. Use an additional long narrow strip of fur to make a flap to cover up the zipper or buttons that run the length of the suit.

Spray the old mask with the black spray paint and set aside to dry. (You might want to have an adult help you with this.)

Sew the fur onto the top of the gloves to make hairy arms. Using the hot glue gun, glue fur onto the top of the old black shoes, completely covering them in fur.

For the head, sew two pieces of fur together to form a hood. Then attach the black mask to the hood.

THE BUSH MAN

PROPS AND PREPARATION

YOU WILL NEED...

- *Dark green fabric, bed sheet, or an old dark-colored beach towel*
- *Leaves*
- *Stapler*
- *Rake*
- *Dark-colored clothing*
- *Friend*

HOW TO DO IT...

Staple leaves on the cloth until it is fairly well covered. You'll have a blanket of leaves when you are finished. Then rake more leaves into a large pile close to the where your guests will pass when they arrive at your haunted house.

Lie on top of the pile of leaves and have a friend cover you with the cloth so you blend in with the leaf pile.

When some unsuspecting visitor wanders by on the way to your haunted house, jump up with a friendly "Boo!"

Did you know that the millions of bacteria at work in a rotting pile of leaves create so much energy that they can actually raise the temperature by dozens of degrees? It's no wonder leaf piles are able to create such nasty creatures. You might want to become a Bush Man (or woman) yourself... there's no end to the fun you'll have with unsuspecting visitors who enter your yard, not knowing what is lurking beneath the nearest pile of leaves.

BOO!

Note: Be careful not to scare small children with this trick.

MAN-EATING CHICKEN

When you get enough mutants together in one place...such as your haunted house...Mother Nature's normal arrangements for who is supposed to be eating whom tend to get confused. That's why, you explain to your friends, there are signs hanging all around saying BEWARE: MAN-EATING CHICKEN. And all those extremely loud and angry chicken noises in the background? Well, the feathered fowl must be getting hungry.

Once you've finally gotten everyone on the edge of their seats, waiting to be attacked at any minute by this ferocious creature, you can let them in on the secret. Lead them around the corner and introduce them to a man calmly sitting there eating...just as the sign said...chicken! What else?

This little prank will help relieve the tension from all of the haunting effects you are showing your guests. What a relief it will be for them when they discover a man eating chicken instead of a man-eating chicken!

THE MUMMY

At first your friends will think you've started a bizarre museum of ancient Egyptian artifacts in your home. Weird hieroglyphics cover the walls of a dimly lit room. A statue of a wild-eyed animal, ready to strike, is poised next to an open coffin propped against the wall. And inside stands the Mummy... wrapped in gauze, with his arms crossed over his chest.

But this guy is not resting in peace. His eyes open and he lurches forward, directly toward your astonished friends.

PROPS AND PREPARATION

YOU WILL NEED...

- *Bathroom tissue*
- *White adhesive tape*
- *White pants, shirt, and socks*
- *Coffin (see page 20) painted with Egyptian hieroglyphics*
- *Brown grocer's paper painted with more Egyptian hieroglyphics*
- *Papier-mâché animal of some kind (you can get a Mexican piñata from a party supply store) painted with...of course...Egyptian hieroglyphics*
- *Paint*
- *Baby powder*

HOW TO DO IT...

The mummy-to-be should be wearing all white clothing. Have him or her stand straight while a friend does the wrapping job with bathroom tissue.

Be careful not to wrap the tissue tightly around the nose and mouth and wrap the head last. Use the adhesive tape to hold the paper in place.

Once the mummy has been wrapped, gently whack him or her a few times with a well-soiled dust mop.

Then, to add some realistic looking mummy dust, apply a few sprinkles of baby powder to the mummy so that he or she passes for being at least a few hundred years old.

Paint hieroglyphics on the coffin, papier-mâché animal, and grocer's paper. Tape the painted grocer's paper to the wall (make sure you get an okay from your parents), and place the rest of the props in position near the mummy's sarcophagus (coffin) to complete this thoroughly frightful effect.

UNSTUFFED SCARECROW

Remember how many pieces the *Wizard of Oz* Scarecrow was in when the flying monkeys were through with him? Well, that scene looks like a Sunday school picnic compared to what happens to the poor scarecrow in this illusion. Parts of this guy are all over the place and a few are missing altogether. But the strangest thing of all is that, even though he's everywhere, his parts seem to have minds...and take actions...of their own.

PERSON HIDES UNDER TABLE SO THAT LOWER HALF OF BODY IS CONCEALED.

ADDED MAKEUP TO STRAW

MAKEUP

ARM SLIPS THROUGH HOLE ON TABLE TOP

PROPS AND PREPARATION

YOU WILL NEED...

■ *Lots of straw and old clothes*

■ *Matching set of old clothes*

■ *Hat and gloves*

■ *2 or 3 draped tables made from 3' x 6' x 1' plywood boards with appropriate-size holes cut in the top with a jigsaw (have an adult help you with this)*

■ *Sawhorses to hold the tabletops*

■ *Old bed sheets to drape the tabletops*

■ *Several assistants*

■ *Appropriate scarecrow makeup*

HOW TO DO IT...

Study the illustrations and you'll see how to put this neat trick together. Through clever use of the holes in the table you can make it look as if parts of the scarecrow have disconnected and disappeared. In fact, body parts are hidden and emerge from beneath the tables.

You can use two or three tables, depending on how fancy you want to get, to make the scarecrow's head, arms, and legs disappear from view. You'll need an extra set of clothes to make the parts look like they belong together.

REAL
HEAD
WITH
MAKE UP.

DRAPE COVERS
PERSON ON KNEES

TOES
WIGGLE

FAKE BODY

LEGS
THRU
HOLE IN BOX

CUT HOLE
IN DRAPE
FOR REAL ARM

TENDONS
MADE FROM
RUBBER BANDS

85

The Zombie Who Rises from the Dead

Even a zombie who's been a lifeless hulk for a hundred years or so isn't completely dead weight. In this wonderful illusion (it's probably the most wonderful thing that ever happened for the poor zombie, anyway), the catatonic creature actually lightens up enough to float from the floor toward the ceiling. It's really something to see, and even more amazing to pull off, this sensational zombie levitation.

PROPS AND PREPARATION

YOU WILL NEED...

- *Person dressed as a zombie with green, lifeless makeup*
- *Second pair of pants, socks, and shoes that match the ones worn by the zombie*
- *2 wooden poles, each about 3' long*
- *Paper towels (3 rolls)*
- *Staple gun (ask an adult to help you with this)*
- *Flat bed sheet*
- *Safety pins*
- *Small cot, or several wooden boxes, for the zombie to lie on*
- *Duct tape*

FROM THE BACK

FROM THE BACK

HOW TO DO IT...

Make a set of "fake legs" for the zombie by stuffing the spare pants with paper towels and inserting a pole in each leg. Stuff the shoes and socks and attach them to the poles with a stapler. Use safety pins to make sure everything holds together on the poles.

To perform this effect, begin with the fake legs hidden behind the cot or boxes where the zombie is laying in his lifeless trance. You, as the mad scientist, explain to your visitors that you have discovered the secret that can raise this zombie from the dead.

Drape the bed sheet over the zombie's body so only his feet are covered. (As you are draping his body, have the zombie lift the fake feet up on the cot so they are sticking out from the sheet, and move his real legs off to the side of the cot). The audience will now see the covered body of the zombie with his head and (fake) feet sticking out from the ends of the sheet.

All the zombie has to do now is lift the fake feet as he slowly stands up behind the sheet. To the audience, it will look like he is floating off the cot into the air.

The zombie must remember to keep his head tipped back, and to hold the fake legs steady. To keep the sheet from falling off and exposing the illusion, a few pieces of duct tape that have been attached to the sheet should be stuck onto the zombie's body as he is being covered with the bed sheet.

To have the zombie float back to the cot, simply have him reverse the process. With a little practice, the effect is really spooky and a great addition to your haunted house.

DON'T LOSE YOUR HEAD!

You probably know people who easily fly off the handle or lose their grip. Well, the fellow in this nasty little scene just can't seem to keep his head screwed on right. The menacing creature that's breathing down his now-open neck isn't helping matters, either.

PROPS AND PREPARATION

YOU WILL NEED...

- *Human mask on a plastic foam wig form*
- *Chair*
- *Beastly monster-type creature (any will do)*
- *Dressed dummy*
- *An assistant*

HOW TO DO IT...

As you can see by the illustration, the trick to this stunt is to have your assistant well hidden behind the chair but positioned so that his arms are free to move naturally, as if they were the dummy's own.

The monster, all in a rage, gives the dummy's head a yank and finds that it quite easily goes its own way. Lovely stuff, don't you think?

87

BLACK WIDOW NIGHTMARE

Black widow spiders are such lovely creatures. Not only do they pack a powerful poisonous bite, they're so vicious they sometimes kill and eat their own mates.

In short, they make great guests for your haunted happenings...especially this large-scale illusion where your audience sees a real human head on the spider. One look and your friends will be bolting for the exits.

HOW TO DO IT...

This illusion requires careful study. It will take some time and effort to gather the materials and build this amazing device, but the effect of a live human head attached to the body of a black widow spider is truly amazing.

The basic idea is build a large box out of plywood and insert the mirror at a 45-degree angle so it hides the girl's body and gives the audience the illusion of being able to see the entire inside of the box.

Actually, the audience really is seeing the reflection off of the mirror in the box, with the girl's head seeming to be a part of the spider.

Begin by having someone help you construct the wooden box out of 3/4" plywood. Make sure the box is strong and the walls are solid. The box should be painted flat black with latex paint.

After the box has been built and painted, have the acrylic mirror (glass is too dangerous) cut so it will fit into the box at a 45-degree angle as shown. Then cut a piece of plywood to fit behind the mirror at the same angle.

Both the mirror and the plywood backing board should be attached to the side walls of the box with wooden strips so they will not move or shift.

Next, make a spider like the one described on page 14, only you must use two larger

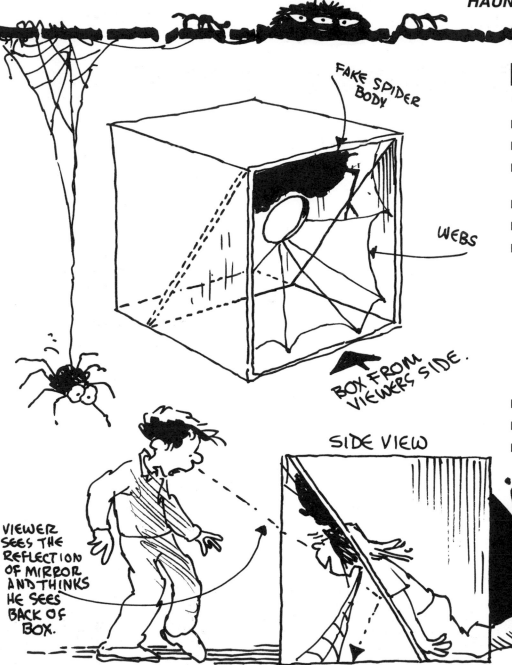

FAKE SPIDER BODY

WEBS

BOX FROM VIEWERS SIDE.

SIDE VIEW

VIEWER SEES THE REFLECTION OF MIRROR AND THINKS HE SEES BACK OF BOX.

PROPS AND PREPARATION

YOU WILL NEED...

- *Several sheets of 3/4" plywood*
- *Nails*
- *A hammer and saw (have an adult help you with these)*
- *Black latex paint*
- *Glue*
- *A square acrylic mirror with a rounded section cut out for the head (Acrylic mirror is available at large hardware stores. You will need to have this cut to fit inside the box at a 45° angle after the box is built. It is best to have an older friend who is experienced at building help you construct this illusion)*
- *Spider web (see page 15)*
- *Oversize spider body (see page 14)*
- *Small plastic spiders on strings*

plastic foam balls (about the size of a large grapefruit and a bowling ball). Cut the balls in half since you will only need to show the top of the spider.

Cover the half balls in black furry fabric (instead of a sock), and paint a red hour-glass-shaped design on the back. Attach the black pipe cleaners, then use a hot glue gun to fasten the spider body to the top of the mirror.

Follow the instructions on page 15 to make a spider web that can stretch over the front of the box.

Have a friend crouch down with her head toward the top of the mirror by the cutout. Since the mirror covers your friend's body, it will look like there is a real half-human,

half-black widow spider spinning a web in your house as guests enter the room.

Keep people a few feet away from the spider (for their own protection of course) but let them talk with the spider to prove that she is real. The spider can tell people that she is an exterminator's nightmare!

To scare the daylights out of people, have another hidden assistant slowly lower small spiders on strings onto the audience from the ceiling. Just watch them jump when the bugs descend.

> *CAUTION: Use only a plastic or acrylic mirror. Glass mirrors are too dangerous.*

A DEATH IN THE FAMILY

When your crazy old aunt finally kicked the bucket, your parents had the brilliant idea of giving everyone a chance to say good-bye to her at home. So you bravely lead your friends into the darkened room, past the strongly scented flowers, right up to the casket. Gloomy funeral music plays in the background. Invite them to join you, leaning in close to get a good look at a real stiff.

But wait...something's not right here. She twitches. Her eyes open in a frightful, empty stare. And she lets out a bloodcurdling, evil laugh as she sits up and reaches for you and your friends. Yikes! This dame ain't dead!

PROPS AND PREPARATION

■ Convince your aunt (or someone else who fits the bill) she will make a great stiff and have her dress formally for the occasion, wearing heavy makeup.

■ Build your aunt's coffin out of cardboard (see page 20.) Place it on a sturdy table covered with a cloth or on some heavy planks over sawhorses.

■ Scent the room with flowers and/or some rose-scented deodorizer.

■ An oscillating fan making the curtains move adds a spooky touch.

■ For a final effect, have a hidden tape recorder playing the death march or some other funeral-like organ music.

AUNT LUCRETIA

FREAKY FRANKENSTEIN

Several thousand volts of electricity to the neck isn't usually what the doctor orders. But when Dr. Frankenstein cranks up the juice to pump some life into his ghoulish monster, your friends will absolutely freak at what happens.

The doctor madly presses buttons and spins dials on his computer, not noticing as his creation wakes up, lets out a growl, and breaks free from the straps that hold him to the operating table. The monster reaches out...first for the scientist, who lets out a bloodcurdling scream...then for your terrified friends!

DANGER HIGH VOLTAGE

BEEP! BEEP! BEEP! BEEP!

GRRR·R·R·R!

ZAP!

PROPS AND PREPARATION

■ Make a "computer" from a large cardboard box. String Christmas lights inside so they flash through holes in the box. Spray-can lids glued on the box look like controls, and dials and levers can be painted on. Connect wires from the computer to the monster.

■ A hidden tape recorder making beeping and electric shock sounds makes for a great effect.

■ A sturdy old wooden table will do for an operating table, or you can make one with heavy plywood or planks over sawhorses. Attach old belts to hold the monster's arms and legs.

■ For the monster and doctor you'll need costumes (ragged clothes for the monster and a dirty lab coat for the doctor) and makeup or masks.

■ Flashing lights on the walls and a DANGER: HIGH VOLTAGE sign complete the atmosphere.

91

ENTER THE SPIRITS

When you invite an all-powerful, all-knowing spirit into your house to share its nasty secrets, no one is safe. Curtains mysteriously move and chains rattle. Objects drift through thin air and the table before you seems to float above the floor. And in a voice from another world, the spirit tells embarrassing, hilarious secrets about everybody present...everyone, that is, except you.

YIPES!

EEEEEK!

PROPS AND PREPARATION

■ You'll need an invisible assistant to rattle some chains and open a window from the outside when contact with the spirit has been made. He or she can also play a hidden tape recorder with the spirit voice reporting secrets (that you dug up in advance by talking with your guests' friends and family) about everyone at the seance.

■ String black thread high across the room that your assistant can use to guide "floating" objects through the air.

■ Set the scene with incense and dim lights. You, the medium, must insert a ruler in both sleeves for lifting the table (see illustration).

■ Insist on absolute silence and complete concentration so that you can force a crack into the world beyond. When your spirit appears, find out its name and be ready with questions that match the secrets that the spirit will share.

Bats in the Belfry

Frightful surprises, disgusting discoveries, and hordes of bats and bugs will make your creepy old attic into a place that will have even your bravest friends screaming and running for cover. Imagine: the rafters are thick with cobwebs and colonies of dangling furry bats. Black lights create a gloomy glow. A blanket of black bugs covers the old furniture and the floor. Glowing eyes stare from the darkest corners. A live captive struggles to break his bonds, while a thumping noise comes from a chain-wrapped trunk. And, yes...that bloody corpse over there really does have a hatchet sticking out of its head!

PROPS AND PREPARATION

■ Cover the floor and furniture with rubber bugs, spiders, lizards, and rats.

■ Fill the room with odd bits of rusty tools and old furniture.

■ Hang fake cobwebs everywhere—the more the better.

■ Make bats from fake fur stuck to black construction paper.

■ Use luminous paint to paint eyes in the darkest corners.

■ Put a tape recorder that plays thumping noises inside a trunk that's wrapped with plastic chains.

■ Black lights make a ghastly, spooky effect.

■ Position a corpse (stuffed dummy) struck on the head by a cardboard or plastic foam hatchet in the corner. Be sure to include plenty of fake dried blood at the site of the wound.

A FRIGHTFUL FEAST

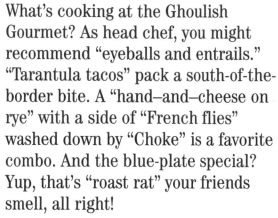

What's cooking at the Ghoulish Gourmet? As head chef, you might recommend "eyeballs and entrails." "Tarantula tacos" pack a south-of-the-border bite. A "hand–and–cheese on rye" with a side of "French flies" washed down by "Choke" is a favorite combo. And the blue-plate special? Yup, that's "roast rat" your friends smell, all right!

PROPS AND PREPARATION

YOU WILL NEED...

- ■ *Tattered, dirty sheets*
- ■ *Art board or cardboard for signs*
- ■ *Marking pens or poster paints*
- ■ *Ping-Pong balls*
- ■ *Spaghetti noodles*
- ■ *Twisted black pipe cleaners*
- ■ *Taco shells*
- ■ *Stuffed rubber glove*
- ■ *Slabs of cheese*
- ■ *Bread slices*
- ■ *Plastic flies*
- ■ *Modeling clay (available from art supply stores)*
- ■ *Lettuce*
- ■ *Hamburger*

HOW TO DO IT...

Tablecloths made of your ripped and dirty sheets help establish a wonderful atmosphere. Signs advertising your most revolting menu selections are a charming touch.

As for the dishes themselves, try painting Ping-Pong balls to make "eyeballs" to go with your "entrails" (spaghetti noodles). Use twisted black pipe cleaners sticking out of taco shells for "tarantula tacos." A stuffed rubber glove and some slabs of cheese between bread slices will do nicely for the "hand and cheese sandwich," and plastic flies work fine for "French flies."

The "lame brain salad" features brain-shaped modeling clay on a bed of lettuce. Surrounded by this disgusting spread, plain old hamburger will pass nicely for a "manburger" made, of course, of the finest "ground Chuck" (may he rest in peace!).

Serving up these dishes is bound to attract a foul crowd. Get things rolling by dressing up a few buddies as ghoulish customers (see costumes and makeup, pages 80 to 83) drooling over a "lame brain salad" or "manburger." They can also lick their chops at the sight of your friends.

THE SNAKE PIT

Getting squeezed to death by a 15-foot python would be a lousy way to croak. But your friends will think watching someone else get scrunched is great grisly entertainment...until, that is, the venomous viper squirts its deadly poison in their direction.

PROPS AND PREPARATION

YOU WILL NEED...

- About 10' of flexible vent tubing for a clothes dryer (available from an appliance store)

- Poster paints

- Plastic foam block about 1' square (available from a hobby store)

- Knife to carve the plastic foam (Have an adult use the knife)

- Straightened coat hanger

- Plastic tube connected to a rubber squeeze bulb (available from a hobby or garden supply store)

- Wicker basket (that looks like it might contain a snake)

- A couple of realistic rubber snakes

HOW TO DO IT...

To build the python's body, begin by painting the vent tubing an appropriate snake-green color. When it is dry, have an adult cut a hole in the side of the tubing in which you can insert your arm to move the snake and squeeze the rubber bulb.

Have an adult carve the plastic foam block into the shape of a viper's head so it fits loosely into the top end of the vent tubing. Paint the head.

Use the straightened clothes hanger to make a hole from the base of the head through the mouth and insert the plastic pump tubing. Connect the tubing to the end of the rubber squeeze bulb filled with water that you can reach through the hole in the snake's body.

Squeezing the bulb will spray your unsuspecting friends with "venom"...but we recommend that you use plain water instead.

Attach the plastic foam head to the python's body.

As guests pass through the snake pit of your haunted house, the giant snake should be coiled around the body of your victim who is controlling the movement of the snake with an arm inside the body. The victim should moan and groan as the snake appears to crush him or her with its body.

A wicker snake charmer's basket and a couple of realistic rubber snakes lying about adds the perfect finishing touch to this slithering, sinister scene.

Aim the snake head over the heads of the audience, and let it rip with a stream of venom to get them moving along quickly.

FINAL RESTING PLACE

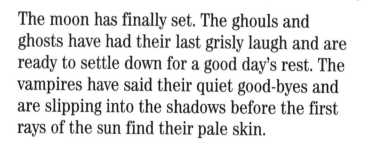

The moon has finally set. The ghouls and ghosts have had their last grisly laugh and are ready to settle down for a good day's rest. The vampires have said their quiet good-byes and are slipping into the shadows before the first rays of the sun find their pale skin.

And your friends? They've had a most unforgettable night of delightful, frightful fun. You had the good sense to take lots of pictures with a camera and camcorder so they'll be able to relive this special event in the days to come.

Thanks to your careful planning, and because you did a good job of including adults in your plans (making sure they checked out all of your exhibits before anyone arrived), everyone had a safe, happy, and frightfully good time.

Nothing left to do now but pick up the pieces...and start planning for your next spooky celebration!!!

'TIL NEXT TIME